LOVE INN THE VIEW

A Natural State Romance

LEAH BREWER

Dedication

This book is dedicated to my late Aunt Clara Dean, or Aunt Dimple as we called her. She had kind eyes, and her demeanor was everything one would expect in an aunt.

Also by Leah Brewer

NATURAL STATE MURDER MYSTERY
To Find a Killer

SEEDS OF FAITH
Keatyn's Journey
Sylvia's Journey
Frankie's Journey
Lottie's Journey

STAND-ALONE BOOK
Petunia 1949

CHILDREN'S BOOK
Charlotte's Birthday Wish

Note From Leah

In To Find a Killer, A Natural State Murder Mystery, we're introduced to the Sharp family as we follow the lives of Detective Tammy Sharp and her mother, Ruby. This time, you'll meet Clara Dean Sharp and her father, Anthony, who are related to Tammy and Ruby. Future Natural State novels will be connected to the Sharp family, so buckle up and get ready to meet these witty, sometimes cheeky Arkansans who have truly won this writer's heart!

Love Inn The View features tender kisses and heartfelt love, avoiding explicit content, steamy scenes, or curses. I hope this charming escape from reality brings you joy, even if just for a little while. Enjoy the adventure!

Chapter 1

Clara

When my best friend, who helped me snag my fiancé, asked for a last-minute favor, I said sure before asking what the favor was.

That's why I'm currently perched in a handcrafted outhouse on wheels with "Potty by Design" painted on the side.

Did I mention I'm also sitting here waiting for two hunky men to try to push me in said outhouse across the finish line quicker than the team beside us?

Not that I'm checking out men, being an engaged

woman. I can't wait to marry Trevor. He planned to be here today to go to lunch with me and Gramma, but he hates beans. Me? Considering I was born and raised right here in Mountain View, Arkansas, I love beans.

I grew up standing on the sidelines, watching people in their own decorated outhouses vying to win the coveted toilet seat trophy. If only things could've been different, I could still call Mountain View home.

I take a deep breath and focus on a woman in a bright red jumpsuit standing behind a square hay bale along the edge of the raceway. Her neon yellow wig reminds me of a porcupine. She yells my name, and my brows raise as I wave back. Wow, she was my seventh-grade Social Studies teacher. With one last wave, she passes in a blur.

Every year, Mountain View has this awesome Bean Fest and Championship Outhouse Race. My best friend Jane was supposed to compete, but she woke up feeling crummy with a stomach bug. Her mom, Abigail, took her to Urgent Care before asking me for a favor.

I said yes without really thinking because I was already nearby. That's when I found out I'd be representing their interior design business in the outhouse race.

Luckily, I had plenty of time to drive from Mountain Home, where I was visiting my gramma, over to Mountain View. And no, they're not the same place.

They are both towns in Arkansas with great views and, for the most part, even better people—except for my eighth-grade algebra teacher, who definitely doesn't make the list.

If only my younger brother Donny could see me now. He'd poke fun and say he can't believe the famous Clara Dean Sharp is participating in an outhouse race.

Okay, so I'm not famous. I just grew up dreaming of someday becoming a famous musician.

It's ironic how Donny is the one in a band now. Oh, and he grew up to be the spitting image of an eighties rock star, and believe me, he uses that to his advantage when booking gigs.

Meanwhile, I look just like our current Miss America. Ha, I'm kidding. With my wild chocolate brown curls, plump lips, and hazel eyes, I can't think of anyone to compare myself to. Not that I'd want to. Just call me an original, one of a kind.

At first, I wondered if Jane was lying to get out of doing it herself, but I've changed my mind. Being in this seat as people yell their support makes me *feel* famous, at least for a moment.

The outhouse lurches to the right, and I squeal. Turns out bumps in the road are not a problem for my drivers. As they speed up, the wind blows in my hair, and I can't stop another smile from springing across my face.

Our competition's outhouse is designed to resemble a phone booth, with a young man inside dressed as Superman. I lean in to glance at them. We're neck and neck.

I scream for the muscular men to run faster. They listen, and the outhouse jerks again as we speed up, working hard to beat the other team.

Where did Jane find these men? Hunky *and* know how to follow directions? I might have considered proposing to one of them if I weren't already engaged.

My heart is beating so fast. The two bearded men pushing the outhouse beside us must've had their Wheaties for breakfast. They smile at me as they sprint ahead. But my hunks are not having it. They kick into high gear and cross the finish line first.

One of the hunks does a cartwheel before grabbing the other one in a bear hug. I can't believe we just won the race! Take that, Donny!

After saying goodbye to my almost-future husband and his friend, I head straight to the nearest pot of beans. My mouth waters at the thought of the rich, ham-flavored beans paired with a sweet piece of corn-bread.

As someone begins to play a folk song, a rush of nostalgia washes over me.

A little later, I slide into my car, aka my baby. It took me over a year to scrape by to save up for a down payment on my dream car: a 2019 Maserati Levante. Now that I have the black beauty to call my own, every bite of ramen noodles I forced down was worth it.

Before driving off, I grab my phone to text Jane as I glance at the bejeweled toilet seat trophy.

I snap a selfie with the trophy and add it to my message.

CLARA

I had fun!

JANE

CLARA

Can I bring you anything?

JANE

New stomach?

CLARA

All out of new stomachs. Anything else?

JANE

Nope. Thank you for today.

CLARA

No problem. I hope you feel better.

JANE

TY

CLARA

When you feel better, I need to know where you found the hunks.

JANE

CLARA! You're engaged!

CLARA

I know that! I'm just nosy

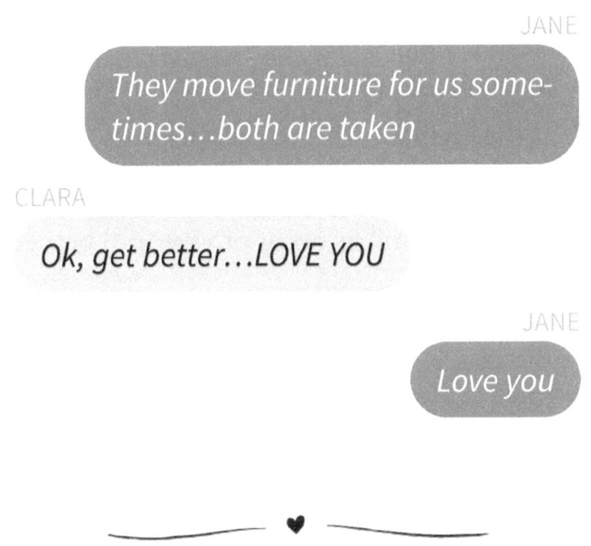

My alarm serenades me with my favorite Taylor Swift song, Gorgeous, first thing Monday morning. I need motivation, a gallon of coffee, and most of all, Trevor.

After getting ready, I grab a bag of croissants at Daily Donuts and head to Trevor's office. He'll be so excited!

My phone buzzes with an incoming call from my mother. Hard pass. She's probably wondering why I came to Mountain View without stopping by to see her. Ever since Dad caught her in an unexplainable situation with my eighth-grade algebra teacher, our relationship has been a bit strained.

I can hardly imagine what drives someone to be

with another person's spouse. Dad said he would've gone to prison if not for me and Donny. Within a week of the incident, as Dad calls it, Mom packed her bags and moved in with Mr. Avery. She said I should look at things from her point of view and begged me to give her new love a chance.

At my high school graduation, she said Mr. Avery, my former algebra teacher turned stepdad, had been through a lot, too. Yeah, it must be exhausting stealing a woman away from her family.

Now, she calls me once a week, and I may or may not answer the call. Dad says I should forgive her and stop holding anger in my heart. Yeah, I'll get right on that.

But in all honesty, I have forgiven her; I just don't care to be around Mr. Avery. I didn't like him as my teacher, and I sure don't like him as a stepdad. And considering how he kicked me out of their house last time I was there, I have no doubt the feeling is mutual.

After dealing with that, I always said I'd find a man who'd never cheat. I've found that in Trevor. Or have I? My heart drops as I peer through Trevor's office window.

Red hair. Red lips. Impossibly tight clothes. Shiny

black heels attached to mile-long legs that are currently so close to my fiancé you couldn't fit a piece of paper between them.

All I can do is stand here. with my hand pressed to my throat as I watch Trevor make out with a redheaded bimbo.

Chapter 2

Clara

As I stare into Trevor's office, everything Dad ever said about forgiveness goes out the window. All my dreams of me and Trevor living in a cute three-bedroom house with a white picket fence fade away as I growl and shoulder my way inside.

Trevor peels his lips off the redhead and looks at me wide-eyed. "What are you doing here, Clara?"

I throw the bag of croissants on his desk. "Surprising you with breakfast," I say, with a humorless laugh. "Surprise!"

The woman's cheeks match her hair as she steps away from Trevor, her bob bouncing as she makes her way past me.

He runs a hand through perfectly styled blonde hair as he steps around his desk. He's way too calm. "Brianna, this is Clara Sharp."

Just Clara Sharp? I see he didn't bother adding that we're engaged.

I direct my burning eyes to *Brianna*, who has one leg in the hallway. I strongly consider blocking the door, imagining the satisfaction of watching her trip as she tries to rush out. However, I ultimately decide against it. Let her leave.

When my gaze circles back to Trevor, he looks mad. Mad? Seriously?

"What are you wearing that for?" he asks, looking down his straight nose at my cream joggers and over-sized Las Vegas Raiders hoodie as he straightens his silky blue tie.

Ever since he was promoted to District Manager at Lombardi Enterprises, he's been dressing like an executive. Currently, I get it, I look like I'm twelve instead of twenty-four. But after wearing power suits for the past couple of years, it feels good to dress down on occasion. Who knew I needed to put on a suit to grab breakfast?

"I thought you were job hunting today," he says as he continues to smooth his tie.

Yeah, I forgot to mention, not only is my fiancé cheating, but I also lost my HR Manager job at Liberty Marketing. After making poor decisions, my boss announced that they were being forced to downsize. A month ago, I got the call that I was no longer needed.

So now, I'm not only not famous but also jobless. And obviously about to be single.

"Plans change." I practically growl, my heart beating fast enough to start a fire. I'm not sure if I want to choke him out or run out of the office and never look back.

"Look, I'm sorry you saw that, but you need to find a job." He narrows his eyes but offers a small smile I guess to appease me. "I can't have you showing up at my office whenever you feel like it."

My blood boils so hot, I think my head will lift from my shoulders. I open my mouth, but nothing comes out. There's no way I will let him see me cry, so I clamp my mouth shut and bite my tongue. Instead of giving him the satisfaction of a response, I spin on my heel and walk out.

Running out of the office and never looking back, it is.

"Clara?" he yells my name, but stays behind his desk, which says a lot. If he were genuinely sorry, he would chase me down. Right? Right.

I wait until I'm on the bottom floor of the high-rise building before I allow my angry tears to flow. How many years have I spent feeling sorry for people who get cheated on? Too many.

Never in my wildest dreams would I have thought Trevor would kiss another woman. And then to act like I'm the one in the wrong? He'd better believe the wedding is off.

The sparkly round diamond engagement ring mocks me as I glance at my hand. Regret for not throwing it in his face consumes me.

I grit my teeth as I pivot on the ball of my foot. I'll show Trevor what he can do with this ring.

But when I turn, my right foot stays firmly in place as if it were telling me to keep going to the car. I suck in a deep breath as pain cracks through my ankle.

I'm going to hit the floor. How could this day get

any worse? My hand reaches out for something to keep from falling. I'm not sure why since there's nothing near me.

"Whoa, there," a masculine voice comes from behind me as someone steadies me by grasping my arm.

When I turn, my gaze locks on the purest blue eyes I've ever seen. If I didn't know better, I'd say they're the same eyes I saw in a Woman's Day Magazine while staying at Gramma's last week.

"You okay?"

I swallow the smart remark and opt for a simple nod. It's not his fault I got engaged to a lying cheater.

He drops his gaze to my ankle. "I'm going to call an ambulance."

That's all it takes for me to find my voice. There's no way I can afford a medical bill at the moment. And I refuse to ask my mom for anything.

"I don't need an ambulance." I scrunch my forehead as my tone comes out sharper than I intended. "But thanks," I add just to be nice.

His brow creases as he attempts to get a better look at my ankle. "Are you sure?"

"Positive," I say, moving my already swelling ankle behind my other leg.

"Let me at least help you to your car."

With a shake of my head, I decline his offer. I don't know anything about this man. Other than he reminds me of a cleaned-up version of the best quarterback ever. And he smells like the black cashmere candle I got Dad for Christmas from Hobby Lobby, with a woodsy scent of vanilla and amber mixed together.

"I promise I'm not a serial killer or anything," he says, pointing at the security guard behind the counter. "Ask him."

I want to make it clear that men should probably keep their distance from me right now—even those who resemble my favorite football player. Instead, I force a smile. "I'll be fine."

I tilt my head and narrow my eyes as I meet this man's gaze. It seems unusual for Archer Banks to be here at this moment. It must be his doppelgänger. I can't imagine him ever wearing a three-piece suit, shaving off his signature beard, or getting a short haircut.

Also, Archer lives in Vegas. I do know that some of his family lives in the state, but for him to be here right now makes no sense. Or does it? He did drop out of football for personal reasons this season, or so I've heard. But I don't have time to worry about who this man is. I have a wedding to cancel.

The Archer Banks lookalike's lips slip into a frown. "I wish you'd let me help you."

"Thanks, but no thanks. Have a good day." A sigh escapes as I walk away. Walk? No, more like limp. Pride totally not intact.

Chapter 3

Archer

I watch as the woman makes her way across the parking lot in her oversized Raiders pullover, sporting my number. My old number, that is. A big part of me wants to chase after her and carry her, kicking and screaming, to get her ankle checked out.

But getting arrested would make for a bad beginning to my first official day as CEO of Lombardi Enterprises. My Italian great-grandfather started a small business almost seventy years ago, which has since evolved into this multi-billion-dollar venture.

We now have resorts in every state. My grandfather became CEO when he turned forty, and then my mother at fifty. After we lost Mom, Dad stepped in for a while, but he had a mild heart attack. Doc said he couldn't handle the pressure. So, I guess it's my duty and honor to step in even though I'm not quite thirty yet.

I hate I had to leave the thing I love most, playing football. But after losing my mom and now my dad's health scare, it can't be helped.

Dad having a heart attack was unexpected. I'm just thankful it was fairly mild. Dr. Meadows told him no more stress, or he may as well plan his funeral. Thankfully, he took it to heart. So much so that he's on his way home from the Maldives after spending two weeks at a resort.

I glance at my watch. I haven't seen Grandfather yet this morning. With it being after nine, I figured he'd be here by now.

I tug at the neck of my white button-up shirt, looking forward to taking it off later. If I could wear t-shirts and sweats to work, I'd do it. I know one thing, this thing is coming off as soon as I get home. I may even burn it.

Almost as if I conjured him up, my grandfather appears at the front door. Even with his tan skin and silver hair, he looks younger than his seventy-five years. I can only hope I look that good when I'm his age.

Betsy, his home health nurse, pushes his wheelchair inside. Her red cheeks tell me he's been running her ragged even though it's early. "Morning, Betsy." I raise a brow as I meet Grandfather's sharp eyes. "What brings you by, Nonno?"

"Betsy insisted we see how your first day is going."

Her sharp intake of breath says otherwise. She wags a plump finger at him. "Mr. Lombardi! You know good and well I did no such thing."

"Well, you should have."

"I started my day with a five-mile run and workout. So, it's going well." My eyes crinkle as I land a mischievous smile on Betsy.

She shakes her head and meets my gaze. "Archer, can you put up with this one while I run to my son's school?"

"Absolutely," I say as I grasp the metal bar on the wheelchair. I pull Grandfather into a wheelie and take off at a sprint. Sure, it's not CEO behavior, but his cackle makes my heart happy.

"Put me down, Cucciolo." He tries to sound firm, but the way he uses my Italian nickname "pup" still warms my heart.

I slow down to a walk. "Where to? My office?"

"Take me to see Trevor."

Of course, he'd want to see Trevor. Without Grandfather, that one would be in the unemployment line. He and Trevor's grandfather had been good friends, and that's how Trevor got the job. And his promotion.

We meet Trevor in the hallway. His face is flushed, and he seems preoccupied. Is that red lipstick on his lips? When he notices us, he shakes both our hands. "Hello, boss. Good to see you both."

Definitely red lipstick.

"You too. How are things going?" Grandfather asks.

"Very well, Mr. L. I'm loving my new role and can't thank you enough for trusting me."

Grandfather nods. "I saw your pretty little fiancée leaving a few minutes ago."

Red blooms up Trevor's neck. "What did she say to you?"

"She seemed upset, but we didn't speak. What happened?"

"We had a small misunderstanding, but it'll work itself out." Trevor smiles.

"Why was she limping?" Grandfather asks.

Trevor's eyes widen. "I have no idea."

Unexpected disappointment fills me as I picture the green-eyed beauty I just met being engaged to Trevor. I had hoped to see her again. But I'm not about to try to steal someone's woman. Not even Trevor's.

No matter that she's clearly a fan. And a very attractive one at that.

Chapter 4

Clara

Jane curls up on the plush sofa in her den and stares at me with those big, brown, puppy-dog eyes. Why is she giving me the face that means she wants something? Couldn't we just have a girls' day of eating random things while watching Sense and Sensibility?

She's the one who demanded to watch something other than my favorite, Pride and Prejudice. Although my goal is to watch Pride and Prejudice one hundred times before I turn thirty, I reluctantly agreed.

Over the past several years, we've watched Pride and Prejudice a total of seventy-five times. The Keira Knightley version is our favorite, having seen it fifty-four times. The second most watched is the one with Colin Firth, which we've watched nineteen times. We watched the 1980 adaptation once and the 1940 version once as well. I know all this because I keep a spreadsheet. I don't play around when it comes to goals that involve Jane Austen.

I sigh. Would asking for my best friend to support me be too much? Since preschool, we've been best friends and survived being separated the summer after eighth grade. I'd hate to ditch her over a movie. Just kidding. I could never ditch her. Weekends at her house kept me sane after my parents' divorce.

She sips pink lemonade and eyeballs me under her lashes. "It's been almost seven months since the name that shall not be spoken cheated on you."

I roll my eyes and pull my fuzzy robe to my neck. "What are you doing? Counting the days?"

"Nope. Clare Bear, I want you to live a little. Go out, have fun, do something—anything!" She tosses a chunk of her golden blonde hair over her shoulder, which then cascades down over her pajamas featuring a picture of Michael J. Fox on the front.

Ever since we started watching eighties movies in high school, Jane has fully embraced that style. Now, she shops at thrift stores and refuses to wear anything modern. I have to admit, she looks cute most of the time.

"I don't want to live a little," I say as I tear up when Miss Dashwood cries over Marianne playing a sad song on the piano. Their father's death was sad enough, but now they're destitute. It's ridiculous if you ask me. And Fanny? Well, she's on my bad side.

Jane gasps before clearing her throat since the gasp didn't catch my attention. I tear my gaze away from the screen and the very handsome Hugh Grant, who plays Edward Ferrars. "Hold on, I meant I don't want a life." I shake my head. "No, not that either. I just want to be alone." There, that sounds better.

"I already know you're having a conversation with yourself in your head, trying to justify what you said. For your information, none of those statements sounded good."

"Hmm. I disagree." I pop a green grape in my mouth. "Look, I have you to keep me in line. I need nothing else, especially since I realized I didn't want to get married anyway."

After I witnessed the kiss that ended my engagement, Jane's mom, Abigail, offered me a job at her design firm. She'd offered after I lost my job, but I had wanted to stay around Cabot to be close to my future husband.

Seeing him with another woman changed my mind rather quickly. I jumped at the offer to freelance as a designer. I love how I can keep my apartment in Cabot and stay here some, too.

It only took three months of online design classes at A-STATE, and I am an official Interior Designer. I'm setting goals again. As if my Pride and Prejudice goal wasn't enough for now, I decided I needed something else to keep Jane off my back.

Last week, Abigail landed a large design job, so she asked me to come for the next few weeks. My former music teacher, Miss Sloan, owns a music store with an adorable two-bedroom apartment upstairs. So here I am in Mountain View for at least the next month, and I feel like I'm finally rebuilding my life.

I've been thinking about rekindling my childhood dream and pursuing a life as a famous musician! I often find myself gazing at the fiddle case I keep propped against my bedroom wall—it's funny how it has become more of a decoration over the years. I'm not quite sure why I've held onto it, especially after I've avoided playing music since Mom and Dad split up. But who knows? Maybe it's time to change that. Maybe Mr. Bingley's release is way overdue. Yes, I named my fiddle Mr. Bingley.

Jane grabs a grape and inspects it before she eats it. "I fixed you up on a blind date."

The piece of Havarti cheese I just chewed up clogs my throat. After taking a few seconds to choke it down, I gulp some water, forgetting all about Sense and Sensibility and Edward. "You did what?"

"You heard me." She pats my back. Like that was gonna help. "Mom's new boyfriend brought his son and nephew by yesterday."

"I am not going on a blind date. It's Thursday night, and I have plans to watch that new Candace Cameron Bure mystery." I pause and raise a brow at her. "And the last time you fixed me up, things didn't go so well."

If not for Jane meeting Trevor through a mutual friend, I would've never dated him. But she thought we would be soooo cute, she had said. Her eyes light up with excitement as she shakes her head, blatantly ignoring my comment. "Trust me when I say you will kick yourself if you don't go."

"I'll pass."

Jane ignores me. "This is the blind date of your dreams. Like for real." When Jane figures out I don't plan to answer, she continues, "They're both gorgeous, so I agreed to an early dinner at The Skillet."

"No."

"Or we can take them to the Ozark Folk Center right now and then picnic by the water."

"Nope. You can take them."

"His name is Chance." She grins and looks off in the distance.

Either she loves the picture of three horses on the wall, or she has a major crush. When this happens, there's no getting through to her.

Looks like I'll be going on a blind date. But that's not the label I'll use. More like a blind ambush.

Chapter 5

Archer

Even though I wish I were on a football field, I'm happy to be outdoors hiking. I breathe in the fresh mountain air with a smile as I step over tree roots crisscrossing the trail. Mountain View is a nice place with great views and has the potential to be a lucrative location for a vacation rental company.

Even though I believe Dad wants to open an office in Mountain View because of Abigail Bennett, a woman he's been on maybe six dates with since meeting her a few months ago, I am happy to be here working behind the scenes on this new project.

"Earth to Archer." My cousin, Chance, snaps his fingers. "Did you hear me?"

"I heard you but chose to ignore what you said." I shrug and continue my trek up the hiking trail.

"I said we need to get ready to meet the girls soon," he says as he brushes a broken spiderweb off his face.

Somehow, Chance developed a crush on Abigail's daughter within five minutes of meeting her. I pause and give him a sidelong glance. "You signed up for a date, not me."

"Please. I like this girl, and she wants to double date before she goes out with me alone." Chance kicks a rock. "I'll owe you one."

Against my better judgment, I agree to a blind date. "Fine. Let's go."

An hour later, just as the sun drops in the sky, we pull into a restaurant called The Skillet that's inside the Ozark Folk Center, a well-known Arkansas State Park.

The Skillet features a wooden ceiling with exposed timber beams and large windows. The walls are adorned with an array of vintage treasures, including a quaint old rocking chair and a variety of brooms.

The atmosphere is warm and inviting, and I wonder if we should incorporate this style into some of our lodges to create a cozier ambiance.

As my eyes wander around the room, I spot Jane at a corner table. She's waving her hands like she's giving a presentation. Her friend has her back to us, so I can't tell what she looks like. Not that it matters. I am *not* looking to date right now.

"Be nice." Chance demands as we approach the table.

"You don't have to tell me how…" I stop mid-sentence as I lock eyes with none other than Trevor's fiancée.

My spine tenses, and I feel too many things contradicting each other. Anger. Attraction. Longing. I've no idea why I feel such strong emotions for a woman I've only spoken to once.

An engaged woman.

Her eyes widen, and she spins around, whispering something to Jane. Yeah, you've been caught, cheater. That's what I want to say. Trevor told me things were well with him and her a few days ago. I asked. Only because I was curious. Nothing else.

Chance grabs my wrist. "What's wrong?"

One glance at his face, and I see the panic. If I'm staying, it looks like I'll spend the evening talking about Trevor because I'm no cheater. "I'll tell you later."

We grab the two empty chairs, and Jane smiles. "I'm so glad y'all made it." She points at her unfaithful friend. "This is my best friend, Clara Sharp."

Chance shakes her hand. "It's nice to meet you, Clara. I'm Chance and this is..."

His words trail off when he sees me burning a hole in the menu with my gaze. The muscles in my jaw tick like crazy. Why am I so angry?

Because I can't stand a cheater.

"Did you hear Jane?" Chance raises a brow. "This is Clara."

I look up and smile thinly. "We've met."

Recognition flickers in her eyes, and red splotches line her cheeks. "You were there that day..." She stops talking and looks away.

"You mean the day you stopped by to visit your fiancé?" The venom oozing from my voice is loud and clear.

She snaps her head around. "What is your problem?"

"I don't know what kind of game you're playing, but I'm not interested in dating an engaged woman." I lean across the table and scowl.

She throws three dollars from her purse on the table and stands. "That's for my lemonade. Jane, I need to talk to you in private." She peers at Chance and says, "Enjoy your evening," then glides past me without a second glance.

Chance watches Jane as she scrambles to reach Clara. He turns to me, narrowing his eyes. "I can't believe you."

"What?"

Just then, Clara's voice carries across the room. "That jerk may resemble my favorite football player, but he is no Archer Banks."

A young, dark-haired waitress chooses that moment to stop by. "Are you guys ready to order? Or do you need a few more minutes?" She smiles, oblivious to the tension at our table.

"We need a few more minutes," I respond, returning her smile. Hearing Clara say I'm no Archer Banks was hilarious. I found myself looking forward to the moment she finds out otherwise.

Jane says something to the waitress before sitting

down and glaring at me as Clara disappears from my view. "I hope our parents don't get married because you're rude."

She wasn't the only one with that hope. At this point, I'm ready to call off the entire thing and go home. Who needs vacation rentals here anyway? "I'm rude? Clara is the one who is engaged."

"What? No, she's not." Jane's look of utter confusion makes me wonder if Clara didn't have a twin.

"Her fiancé works for me. So, I think I know."

Jane shakes her head. "Why would you say that? Clara broke up with Trevor months ago."

"He told me just last week that the wedding planning is going well," I say as I lay the menu on the table.

"He's a liar. She saw him kissing another woman in his office last October. She returned the ring the next day."

"That makes no sense. Why would he lie?"

"Who knows why men do anything?" Jane says with another glare.

I wasn't sure whether she was referring to Trevor or me. One thing I knew for certain: I probably just ruined any chance I had with the woman who's been haunting my dreams for the past seven months.

Chapter 6

Clara

Normally, I would slow down to admire the seven deer grazing in a grassy area as I pull out of The Skillet's parking lot. However, my blood is hot right now, making it hard to appreciate the view.

I force myself to think of good things, like how the Ozark Folk Center, where the restaurant is located, has always been one of my favorite state parks. I grew up listening to music and even learned to play the fiddle here. I still remember the moment I named my brand-new fiddle Mr. Bingley; it was during a festival at this very location. My first job was supposed to be at The Skillet, but that plan fell apart after we moved.

I even got my first kiss here. I was ten when a boy who'd been here on vacation with his family pecked me on the cheek. It was after I'd played a song on Mr. Bingley. My cheeks were flushed, and I probably smelled, but he said I was the prettiest girl he had ever seen before he ran away. I didn't think so at the time, but he was a cute boy. The car behind me honks, jarring me out of my thoughts.

As I drive three minutes to my apartment, I decide not to let that rude, egotistical jerk bother me. It was a strange coincidence that the same man who offered to help me to my car the day I caught Trevor cheating was the same person Jane wanted to fix me up with.

Even stranger is the fact that I've had a celebrity crush on his lookalike for years. Archer Banks is arguably the best quarterback ever. His hair is longer, and he seems nice. Unlike Mr. Jerks Unlimited.

Jane will forever be banned from fixing me up on blind dates.

He must know Trevor. How else would he think I'm engaged?

Ugh, quit thinking about him!

A grin spreads across my face when I get out of my car. A group is in a circle, jamming in the park next to my apartment. I wonder if I should release Mr. Bingley from his prison as I drift over to where they're playing. Nah, the way my luck has been going, I've probably forgotten how to play.

After a few songs, my phone buzzes with a text from Jane.

I slip my phone into my back pocket and hyperventilate. Did she say Archer? After retrieving my phone and rereading the text, it's confirmed.

More hyperventilating as I pass the white picket fence in front of the music store. I lower myself onto a bench and take a few slow breaths.

Some surprise! I feel like I just walked in on my fiancé kissing another woman, part two.

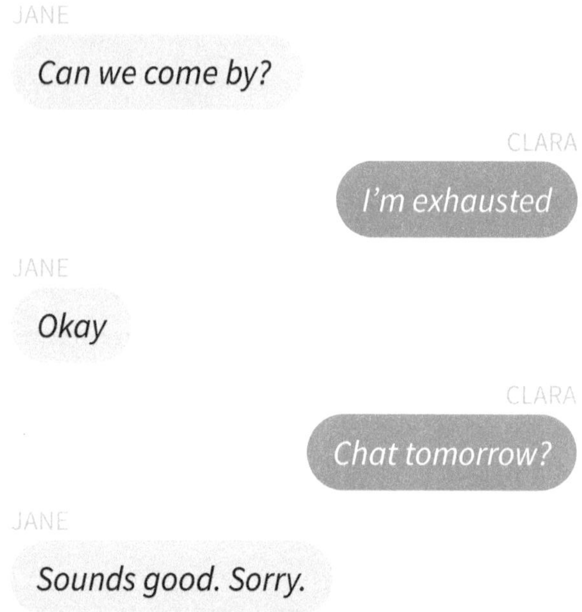

I liked the message before putting my phone in my bag. With a groan, I take it back out, contemplating sending Jane another message. But I don't know what to say. First of all, I'm amazed that I met Archer Banks. Secondly, I hate that he's not the nice guy I always envisioned, but that's not Jane's fault. Thirdly, I hope to never see him again. On or off the field.

I type a message to Jane before going up the stairs to my adorable apartment above the music store.

After finishing my nightly routine, I cozy up in bed

and check my phone. Jane laughed at my message and told me she loves me too.

I close my eyes and force a picture of Archer Banks out of my head.

Chapter 7

Clara

Armed with two cups of coffee from Sasquatch Cave, I pull into Jane's driveway. Even though it's Friday, Jane took off work to go horseback riding. I am so ready.

I walk in without knocking and get five feet before I come to a fast halt.

Jane's mother, Abigail Bennett, hoots a laugh at something Archer stupid Banks is saying.

She swivels and meets my gaze, her eyes sparkling. "Clara! It's so good to see you," she says as she stands, heading my way.

"Morning, Abigail," I reply as a rock forms in my stomach.

"I'm off to work. See y'all later," Abigail says before walking outside.

Jane and Chance come out of the kitchen, and Jane runs after Abigail. "Bye, Mom," she says as the door slips shut behind her.

I know Jane like the back of my hand, and right now she's stalling.

The enemy is sitting in her living room, and she's scared to face me.

She better be.

Archer runs a hand through his hair and meets my gaze. He's wearing a navy button-up with army green shorts and brown loafers. That's good. At least that means Jane has no plans to invite him and Chance for horseback riding.

I narrow my eyes before averting my gaze. His looks have no bearing on how I feel about him.

Not at all.

Amusement darts across his face. "I guess you didn't know I'd be here this morning?"

I shrug. "Makes no difference either way."

He snorts a laugh and looks at Chance, who plops down beside him.

Chance clears his throat and trades a glance with Archer before his gaze moves to me. "Thanks for letting us tag along today."

My eyes blink a few times as I'm racking my brain for a response. There's no way Jane would invite them without at least asking me.

No way.

I storm to the door and yank it open. Jane jumps like a frog trying to outrun a snake.

Abigail is already gone, so that means Jane's been out here hiding. "Please tell me you did not invite Archer Banks to go horseback riding with us."

Jane's face beams with nothing but guilt, and I know there *is* a way she would invite them without asking me. "I'm doing this for you."

I shake my finger at her. "For me?"

"Yes, you." She leans her head back and looks at the sky. "If you let Archer Banks walk out of your life without getting to know him, I know you'll regret it."

I frown. "I don't know about that."

"Well, I do. Please let them go with us." Her lower lip trembles as she meets my fiery gaze.

My temples pound as a sudden headache hits me. "Fine, Jane."

She grabs my wrist. "Are you mad at me?"

"No, I'm not mad," I sigh. "I just have a headache."

"You haven't had your coffee yet, have you?"

I shake my head no.

She loops her arm through mine as she leads me inside. "Come on, then."

Archer glances our way, his gaze settling on Jane. "I forgot I have to be somewhere this morning, so you three have fun." He breezes past me and out the door, leaving nothing but a woodsy fragrance behind.

I ignore the fact that he makes me think of a cool summer rain on a scorching day.

Sipping my coffee, I silently congratulate myself for running him off. With any luck, this will be the last time I run into Archer Banks.

Jane shoots me a disapproving glare, and I respond with a grimace. "What?"

She taps her chin, looking puzzled. "I really think you're your own worst enemy."

Unfortunately, I cannot disagree.

— ♥ —

After coffee and a couple of Advil, my day improved, and I actually had fun with Jane and Chance. He seems to be a nice guy. Unlike his cousin.

I drop Jane off with Chance and rev up the engine, ready to head to my rental. Friday nights in Mountain View are electric—there's always something amazingly musical going on.

I can't wait to settle onto the porch, soaking in the old school sounds of whatever band will be at the courthouse square. It's going to feel just like old times, even if I'm flying solo this time around.

With Mom and Dad divorced and my brother Donny off carving his own path, I might be alone, but that doesn't dim my spirit. Jane is with Chance, but who cares? After the whirlwind that was Trevor, I've finally rediscovered my spark, and life is good.

At the apartment, I hum as I go inside, shower and slip on sweatpants and an oversized t-shirt. I bite my lip as I look for something to eat. After I grab a banana, I go downstairs as I dial Donny's number.

He answers on the first ring. "Hey, Sis!"

"Hey, what you doing tonight?" I ask, lowering myself onto the bench on the front porch.

"Getting ready to go on stage!" The excitement in his voice brings a smile to my face.

"Where are you?"

"Des Arc. They're having a couple of bands play on the river."

"That's awesome! Well, I'll let you go so you can get ready. Love you."

"Love you! Call me later if you want."

"Okay."

I guess I'll tell him about meeting Archer Banks some other time. Unless I decide to forget that man exists.

As if.

Chapter 8

Archer

It's not normal for me to skip breakfast. Especially when the owner of The Inn at Mountain View makes such mouth-watering food. But I don't eat when I'm aggravated. I step outside, only stopping when I reach a rocking chair.

I lean back into the chair and glance around the yard. A little blue bird twitters by the fragrant array of flowers lining the cobblestone walkway. Knowing I need to get a grip, I close my eyes and force Clara Sharp out of my thoughts.

That works out to a total of forty-five seconds before my mind replays what I heard her say to Jane yesterday. *"Please tell me you did not invite Archer Banks to go horseback riding with us."*

I don't know what her problem is. Honestly, I thought she was my biggest fan, considering she had my jersey on the day we met. Guess I was way off. Maybe I'm losing my appeal now that I'm no longer playing football. I'd love nothing more than to be back in Vegas training for the next game. Nothing.

By the time Chance finishes breakfast, I've worked myself up. My jaw is ticking, I'm drumming my fingers on the arm of the rocking chair, and I want to knock the patriotically decorated rooster over.

Chance follows my line of sight and grins. "Man, you look like you want to fight that rooster."

I grunt, and he continues. "That rooster ain't never done nothing to you. I think your real problem is Clara Sharp."

With a groan, I drop my head in my hands. "I don't even know her."

He waves like what I said doesn't matter. "You want to, though."

My fingers clutch the rocking chair arms before I

bolt upright. "I disagree."

"Say what you want, but I know you. You're into her," he accuses, bouncing on his toes.

"Whatever," I say as I hustle down the steps past the rooster that I may just owe an apology to. "Let's walk around. Dad woke up with a headache, so he's still asleep."

"Lead the way."

We make it as far as the gazebo across the street from the inn before I stop. "Clara Sharp is rude, so why would I want to get to know her?"

He chuckles. "Jane told me Clara thinks you're rude."

My mouth falls open. "I don't know why."

Chance has the nerve to look shocked. Before I can demand to know why, my phone rings. I smile and answer on the first ring. "Morning, Nonno."

"Good morning, Cucciolo. How are things going in Mountain View?"

I resist the urge to tell him about how rude Clara Sharp is. There's no reason to bring her up. Instead, I say, "going great. I think this is a prime location for a vacation rental office."

We talk for a few minutes as Chance and I continue

down the sidewalk. Once we round the corner by Urban Forge, we come face to face with Jane and Clara. I roll my eyes as I enter the double doors.

As soon as Grandfather and I end our call, my eyes scour the space, and I'm impressed. A massive four-poster bed gets my attention right away. The details are intricate, and I have no doubt whoever made this takes pride in their work.

Chance joins me beside the bed, a smile that would work well on an alligator shining brightly. Unease travels down my spine. That smile means he's happy about something. And whatever it is, I can guarantee it's nothing good for me.

Jane comes inside with Clara, who takes a few faltering steps in my direction before taking off toward the opposite side of the room. Figures.

"The girls are gonna walk around with us if that's okay," Chance says, happily ruining my plans for the morning. I don't bother answering.

The sales representative comes over and tells me about the bed, which I plan to purchase and possibly have shipped to Little Rock. I leave with her card and promise to return to finalize the details.

Chance and Jane walk hand in hand, like they're a

couple. Meanwhile, Clara does her best to ignore me. This is ridiculous.

I clear my throat. "So, do you live in Mountain View?"

Clara side-eyes me, her hazel green eyes sparkling like the sun hitting a butterfly's wings. "No." is her clipped response.

"If you don't want to walk around with me, you should've said so. It's not like I invited you." Even though my backbone stiffens, I sprint ahead, disappearing inside a flea market. There's no way I'll put up with her attitude all day.

No thanks.

Later that evening at Abigail's, I catch Jane narrowing her eyes at me. My dad and Abigail are in the den watching a movie, and for some reason, I'm here as well after Dad insisted I get to know Abigail and Jane. They'll probably last another month or two, so what's the point? If not for him, I'd be at the inn, curled up in bed getting some much-needed sleep.

I wipe a piece of invisible lint off my joggers. "What's on your mind, Jane?"

She looks at me for another few seconds as she lounges in a patio chair. "Just wondering why you never apologized to Clara for accusing her of being a cheater."

If I were honest, I'd admit that I've wondered the same thing more than once this afternoon. Maybe it's because she jumbles my brain every time she's near, and I can't think straight. I've never been this attracted to a woman before.

"Call her and I'll apologize."

She shrieks as she propels herself up. "Oh, you'll need to do better than that. Come on, I have an idea."

I follow behind Jane and Chance, wondering if this is what it's like to have a bossy little sister.

Chapter 9

Clara

Archer Banks is a classic spoiled celebrity. I can't believe I wasted so much time watching him play football. He's rude and mean, and I don't like him at all.

Completely ignoring the fact that I've been a little bit mean myself, I lower my head onto my steering wheel after I park at my rental.

I'm so ready for his perfect blue eyes and beautiful face to stop dominating my thoughts. He is the most stunning man I've ever seen. But looks ain't everything.

My phone buzzes. I unglue my head from the steering wheel and crack my eyes open.

JANE

Are you busy?

CLARA

That depends.

JANE

We have pizza…

CLARA

You and Chance?

JANE

And Archer…

We're coming over.

My head tells me no, but my stomach disagrees. Maybe my heart does, too.

Not that I intend to pursue anything with a man who is so blatantly full of himself.

But I have another opportunity to get to know Archer Banks, my football hero, and I would regret passing that up.

I think.

JANE

Promise you won't regret it!

My heart races as I hurry up the stairs two at a time to grab the clothes I left on the sofa this morning.

As I rush past the sink, I notice a few dishes I'd also left behind. Making a mental note to start cleaning up in the mornings, I throw the clothes on the bed in the extra bedroom and head back to the kitchen, nearly tripping over my feet.

Luckily, I finished loading the dishwasher before the front door bursts open.

"Honey, we're home!" Jane's singsong voice carries up the stairs.

"This place is cool," Chance says when they make it to the second floor.

I agree. The dark stairs flow into a white wrap-around barrier in the kitchen. The stove sits in an alcove below a window on one side of the staircase. The refrigerator, sink, and cabinets are directly in front of the stairs. But the real standout is the rack of pots and pans hanging from the ceiling above the staircase. It has to be the most unique place I've ever stayed. Too bad I won't be moving here, or I'd make an offer to buy the apartment.

Jane, Chance, and the extra-large pizza disappear into the living room, leaving Archer and me alone. He's sporting navy shorts and a baby blue polo. I swallow and look at the floor.

The same man I've watched play football for the past five years is in my kitchen. He's a jerk, but he's still here, nonetheless. His hair is short now, and his beautiful beard is gone, but it's him. I can't believe I didn't recognize him the day I ran into him at Trevor's office.

He clears his throat. "I owe you an apology."

"Okay."

"What does that mean?" He furrows his brow as he slips his hands into his pockets. "Do you accept my apology or not?"

"You said you owe me an apology, which is not an actual apology." I cock my head and meet his gaze.

"You have got to be kidding me." He bites his bottom lip and removes both hands from his pockets, holding them palms up. "I am so sorry for what I said at the restaurant and for being rude earlier today. Please accept my humble apology."

"Accepted. Thank you." I somehow maintain a blank expression even though my heart has successfully completed about fifteen cartwheels.

Jane claps her hands and gives her best impression of Mrs. Bennett. "Oh, thank the Lord, I thought this might never happen!"

I roll my eyes as I follow her into the living room. She sits beside Chance on the sofa positioned between two windows. I choose one of the two identical rocker recliners flanking the sofa. Archer lowers himself into the other one and glances at the TV.

Jane turns on Sixteen Candles. "I vote we watch a movie while we eat. Sound good?"

I groan. "Are you really planning on forcing us to watch Sixteen Candles?"

"Yes, I am. Now, let's eat our pizza before it gets cold."

Archer looks at me and grins. My heart may or may not explode in my chest and I can't help but grin back.

Oh boy. This is not good. With those dimples, Archer Banks is a heartbreak waiting to happen. I watch him from under my brow. It's hard to believe he's in my living room. And without a doubt, this man is perfect in the looks department. Stunning.

Beautiful. Manly.

But not for me. The last girl he was seen on a date with is a supermodel, for crying out loud. It's better to keep things cool. I inwardly laugh at how absurd I sound arguing with myself about the possibility of dating, my gaze darts to Archer, *him*.

After two slices of meat lover's pizza, I grab my latest book by Martha Rodriguez and hold it so Archer can see the cover. I bite my tongue to keep from laughing out loud as his eyes widen when he reads the title, "Lord, Change Him or Kill Him: and right now, I don't care which."

Chapter 10

Clara

Am I at the wrong house? My best friend, a strict eighties fashion girl, is dressed in a Poodle skirt.

"What are you wearing?" I blink at Jane as she twirls around. "That's not your classic eighties outfit."

She flips her hair across her shoulder. "Nope. I decided to wear another decade to church this morning. Just this once."

Abigail, Jane's mom, walks into the room, shaking her head. Her perfectly styled, sleek blonde hair stays in place, looking silky smooth. She may be in her forties, but she's putting off young Heidi Klum vibes. "I don't know what's got into her."

Jane looks at her phone and cocks her head as she taps on the screen. "Hey. I've been meaning to ask if you're kin to someone named Tammy Sharp? I saw an article about her last night."

"Not that I know of. Why?" I move closer to Jane, peering at the phone screen.

"Check this out. She saved her mom from a kidnapper and ended up finding a killer last October." She gasps and turns toward me. "She also killed him."

"Really? Let me see."

Jane hands me her phone. "She's from Pocahontas. You sure you don't know her?"

"I don't. Let's call Dad." I press the FaceTime button on my phone, and within seconds, Dad's smiling face pops up on the screen.

"Hey there, peanut."

"Hi, Dad. Quick question. Are we related to Tammy Sharp?"

"Tammy? Yeah, she's family, a few branches down the family tree. Why do you ask?" He raises an eyebrow.

"Did you know she caught a killer last year?"

"I heard a little about that," he replies, adjusting in his seat with a smile.

"How could you not tell me? That's such a big deal!"

"Oh, it just slipped my mind with everything else you had going on," he chuckles lightly.

"Why have I never met her? I feel like we've been missing out."

"You know how busy life gets. Plus, she moved to Atlanta and was a homicide detective there for a few years."

"I really want to meet her. It's so crazy that she lives nearby and we've never run into each other."

"Well, you actually met Tammy and her mother, Ruby, once at a family reunion. You were little, though." He chuckles softly as he rubs his graying goatee.

"I'd like to meet them now. Tammy saved her mom from a murderer."

"Tell you what, I'll see what I can do."

"Thank you, Dad."

"Have a good day, darlin'."

Jane pops her head into the screen. "I miss you, Papa Sharp."

"I miss you, too, Jane."

We end the call just as the doorbell rings. Probably the neighbor's kid who has been riding to church with Abigail since he was in preschool.

I head into the kitchen, a separate room from the rest of the house. The light blue patterned wallpaper stands out against their all-white design. "Jaaaaane, I thought you were making smoothies this morning."

"Oh, crud, I forgot. We have time to go out for breakfast." She pokes her head into the kitchen.

"That's fine as long as you're not trying to set me up on another date." I open the fridge, scanning the shelves for a snack. "I have no intention of ever seeing Archer Banks again."

Jane clears her throat. Not a regular, I have something I need to cough up throat clearing. More like you've just said something you shouldn't have in front of someone you shouldn't have type of throat clearing.

I take a quick inventory of what's in the fridge and wonder if I can fit inside or not.

As I'm contemplating, the person I planned on not seeing again peers at me over the fridge door. "Sorry to disappoint you, but us not seeing each other is going to be a slight problem."

He smells like wood and trees and streams and everything crisp and fun, and I hate it. You know what else I hate? The fact that I have a strong desire to wrap him in a hug and bury my face in his neck.

"What are you doing here?" I stand and tuck a few pieces of hair behind my ear, my eyes locking in on how his light pink polo flows perfectly with navy slacks and dark brown dress shoes. He's mastered the Hallmark leading man vibes look.

"Abigail invited us to church."

Of course, she did. Shame courses through me with the thought as I fan my face. She absolutely should have invited them. I should have, too. With a deep breath, I relax my shoulders and smile. "I'm glad."

Confusion etches across his face. "Really? Because it didn't sound like that when I walked in here."

Lifting my gaze to the ceiling, I inwardly groan. "I'm sorry about that. What I said was mean."

The side of his mouth quirks upward. "It's forgotten."

"Great," I say, shutting the fridge.

"Great." He mocks me. But he looks adorable doing it. As soon as he meets my gaze, my breath catches.

Oh boy, my heart is in trouble. Big time.

Chapter 11

Archer

After a quick lunch once church was over, Jane decided to take us exploring around Blanchard Springs. Our first stop is Blanchard Springs Cavern, which has me in awe.

We take an elevator ride deep into the cavern and are now touring a place that could be the main setting for a superhero movie.

I'll admit I had my reservations when Jane announced we were visiting a living cave, but this place is magnificent. It appears to be large enough to hold several football fields.

I pause and take in the view, making a mental note to reach out to my coach. The team would love to tour this place.

A person at the visitor center mentioned that the cavern features almost every type of calcite formation you'd find in limestone caves. This place is a must-visit for anyone traveling in the vicinity.

My eyes seem to have a mind of their own as my gaze keeps landing on Clara. She's a few steps ahead of me with her dark curls pulled into a bun. There's one lone curl hanging over her navy-blue sweater that I long to touch.

She pulls the sweater around her neck and says something to Jane.

A jolt of jealousy travels through my body. What am I jealous of? Clara talking to Jane? For some reason, I wish she were talking to me instead. I want her to look at me. Smile at me. Something to show me she knows I'm alive.

I swallow and glance around at the massive formations hanging from the ceiling.

A salamander darts in front of Clara, and she leans down, reaching her hand out toward it. It scurries away, and she turns her head, smiling at me. Well, maybe not directly at me, but her face lights up with happiness.

And me? Well, my heart just skipped several beats.

Given how she barely spoke to me at lunch, I'm surprised that Jane managed to get her to go with us. Well, she's here but continues to ignore me.

At least she doesn't have that book with her. What was that about anyway? Surely, she's not reading a book about killing men.

Don't women do things to get under our skin? I know my ex was good at trying to keep me on edge. Maybe that's what Clara was doing with that book.

The wet stone, which we've been instructed not to touch, smells fresh. I want to run my fingers down it, but the man giving the tour has already gotten onto the man behind me for doing it.

Clara walks side by side with Jane while Chance stands with me, looking just as awestruck.

Jane looks over her shoulder. "The cave is constantly changing and growing. That's why it's called a living cave."

"That makes sense," Chance says.

We finish the hour-long tour and head toward a

waterfall a few minutes away.

Once out of the vehicle, green trees and bushes fill both sides of the boardwalk on the short walk to Mirror Lake Falls. The scenery features rock formations and lush trees along the mountainside.

The air is so crisp, I contemplate leaving Chance, Jane, and Clara behind to find a longer trail. But I'm looking forward to seeing the waterfall I hear up ahead.

I glance around, and Clara meets my gaze. She quickly looks away, but not before I catch a flicker of interest in her green eyes. She falls back close to where Chance and Jane are gazing at each other, and they begin a conversation.

Little Miss Clara can pretend she isn't affected by me, but her eyes say something else. A grin the size of one of the tree trunks to my right crosses my face.

Since she's not with Trevor, maybe I should make up for how I acted like a first-class jerk when we met at that restaurant. I'm not looking for a serious relationship, and I bet Clara isn't either, after her recent called-off engagement. Maybe we could spend time together on a more casual basis.

Proud of my good idea, I make a beeline for Clara,

who stands at an overlook staring at the ruins of an old mill.

I notice tears on her lashes. "Are you okay?"

"The last time I was here, my parents were still together. We walked the trail up to the old mill." She gives a one-shoulder shrug. "I know it's silly for me to get emotional about that. I mean, I'm a grown woman."

"That's not silly at all." I get lost in the sounds of the waterfall as memories of my childhood dance around my mind. "I lost my mom nearly four years ago, and I still have a hard time dealing with the empty space she left behind."

Her eyes widen. "I'm so sorry. Here I am, getting upset over nothing. You must think I'm a little extra."

"Not at all." An intense desire to pull Clara into my arms strikes me. I shake it off. There's no way I should be having such a reaction. If only she knew what I was thinking. She'd probably run. "So, what was that book you were reading last night about?"

Her lips twitch, and I can tell she's fighting off a smile. "I met the author at an event a few months back. She was nice, and I love the title…" She bites her bottom lip before a sweet-sounding laugh breaks out.

"I'm curious, does the man change or get killed?" I ask as we continue walking until we reach the waterfall.

"Who?" She bites her lip again, and I swallow as I zero in on her full, pink lips.

I drag my eyes to the waterfall before she catches me staring. "The character in the story. Does he die?"

She grins, a spark of mischief dancing in her eyes. "Oh, I'm not finished yet, but it's about three women who have abusive husbands, so we'll see what happens."

I cock my head and lift my left brow. "Be sure to let me know."

"Absolutely," she replies, her tone light. "I'll even loan you the book if you'd like. You can mail it to me when you're finished."

"Nah, you can just tell me the highlights."

"What if we don't see each other again?"

I lean close, and the warm, sweet fragrance of vanilla and peaches envelop me. "Oh, believe me, we'll see each other again."

Clara raises a brow, a small smile tugging her lips. "I'm not so sure about that." She turns to Jane as she and Chance join us.

Jane removes her sunglasses and caps her eyes on the waterfall flowing from gorgeous water surrounded by more trees and greenery than I've seen in a long time.

"No matter how many times I see this view, I still can't get over how gorgeous it is," Jane says.

Chance entwines his fingers with hers and stares at her like a love-sick puppy. "It is beautiful."

We decide to continue to the Blanchard Springs Trailhead, which is a few minutes down the road. Once there, we embark on another walkway, but this one is made of stone and rock.

The stream that runs along the trail mesmerizes me as we take our time to enjoy the view.

Once we reach the end of the walkway, there's another waterfall flowing directly out of the side of the mountain. Large rocks cover the area, and steps lead down to the water.

A sign that says Entrance To The Spring Is Prohibited makes me want to enter the spring, but I won't. I'm not a lawbreaker, after all.

With a smile, I glance at Clara. "Want to walk to the water with me?"

She hesitates, looks at Jane, and then shrugs. "I guess."

What is her deal anyway? Most women at least attempt to flirt with me when they can. Clara has been with me all morning, trying to pretend I don't exist the whole time.

It's time I up the ante. "What are you doing tonight?"

"Why?" she asks as she stares up at the sky. A hawk flies past and out of sight.

"I thought you and I could grab dinner and watch a movie." The smile I put on her would undoubtedly get her to say yes.

Her forehead creases, and she frowns. "Thanks, but I'll pass."

My heart stops at her words. She'll pass? "Why? I know you find me attractive."

"Excuse me?" Surprise etches across her face, and she crosses her arms.

"I can tell." I insist, a hint of confidence creeping into my tone.

"You are something else," she says, her lips tugging downward.

"Well, don't you?" I challenge, leaning in slightly.

"It takes more than looks to be attractive."

"What is that supposed to mean?" I ask, my curiosity piqued. "Are you still into Trevor or something?"

She spins around abruptly and gets in my face, close enough that I can tell she has a piece of watermelon gum in her mouth. "I would never marry a cheater."

"I would never cheat on you," I whisper.

She shakes her head, and her expression softens momentarily before she continues, "You'll never get the chance. Starting Monday, I will be immersed in designing a new office downtown and have no time to date anyone."

My heart races in my chest. I can hardly believe my luck. The only reason I'm in Mountain View is to open up a new vacation rental office. And I hired Abigail's design firm to work for me. Clara will be working on my design!

She marches past me and into the shallow water, stopping on a large flat gray rock.

Instead of letting Clara know she's breaking the rules, I follow her, trying to keep my excitement in check as I close the distance between us.

Suddenly, she spins around, her eyes sparkling with energy, and I don't have enough time to stop before colliding with her.

In that split second, her foot slips, and we both lose

our balance. We tumble into the deeper but still rocky water with a splash that sends cool droplets flying in all directions.

The water is cold against my skin, but I can't focus on that as I glance at Clara. All I can think about is the thrill of excitement swirling in my belly.

I guess I am a lawbreaker, after all. But it was definitely worth it.

Chapter 12

Clara

Archer Banks has his arms around me. This is not how I imagined things going with us. That's all I can think of as we fall into the water.

Somehow, he ends up underneath me, taking the brunt of the fall. Still, the water is cold, and I shiver. So why am I considering how it would feel to kiss him?

Because I'm a glutton for punishment.

He grins at me, and I know without a doubt that he knows. He can tell I have had a crush on him since I first saw him on the football field. He can tell I used to doodle his jersey number 17 in my planner.

Is it possible for him to know this? Rationally, I know it's not. But I'm not being rational right now. I'm literally lying in Mirror Lake Falls on top of Archer Banks.

This can't be happening. I would rather be anywhere else than here.

Liar.

Okay, maybe a part of me has dreamed of meeting Archer and falling instantly in love, but that was when I was a couple of years younger. And this will never be that.

I'll settle for my daydreams where things work out like a fairytale, and we live happily ever after.

Jane and Chance rush over, and she helps me to my feet as I swallow a mouthful of spring water. "What happened?"

"We slipped." My teeth chatter, but I manage to throw a dirty look at Archer.

Archer steps out of the water and rings his shirt out. My eyes double in size before I quickly slam my lids shut. How does he look like a model for Tropic Hawaiian suntan lotion? I probably look like a wet weasel.

A couple come from the other direction, stopping to gawk at us. I wave and they wave back before stopping near the frothy cascade of water falling out of the rocks.

As we walk up the rock steps, Jane pulls a tissue out of her backpack and hands it to me. "You have a little something on your nose," she whispers.

"What is it?"

She looks at me with a round-eyed expression. "Just wipe it off."

I'm frantically wiping, but don't see anything. "What is it?" I ask again.

She blows her breath out. "It was snot, okay?"

I. Am. Dead. Did I say fairytale earlier? This is more like the dark and twisted version where I wet my pants, and he laughs me to scorn.

How did I not know I had snot on my nose?

I take off speed walking toward the parking lot. And safety.

Archer tugs at my arm. I keep walking. He catches up and stops in front of me, twisting around so we're face to face. "You okay?"

"Sure. You?" I keep my head down. I will never look him in the eyes again. Luckily, I won't have to because

I figure he'll be leaving soon.

"I'm good." He falls behind, seeming to get the hint that I am mortified and want some space.

As we make the short trek to Jane's purple Jeep, my stomach knots up, and I have a strong desire to run away as I glance in the side mirror.

Did I say I looked like a wet weasel? No, it's much worse than that. I resemble my great-grandfather in the pictures of him from Vietnam. Yes. I look like a man.

I run my hands through my curls. Who cares what Archer Banks thinks anyway? It's not like I'm trying to impress him. Things would never work out between us, and I am not looking for a simple fling.

Unlike him, I'm not bored trying to pass the time by toying with someone's feelings. I'm ready to find happiness ever after, no matter how long it takes.

Going forward, I will only date serious men who are ready to commit to a long-term relationship. So, not Archer Banks.

He's so self-centered that he never once thought I could not find him attractive. Yes, okay, I definitely find him attractive, but that's none of his business. Besides, I'm only here to do a job, and that doesn't include dating the hottest man who's ever graced my presence.

It's not like I'll ever see him again, anyway.

Chapter 13

Clara

First thing Monday morning, Jane and I stand in line at Sasquatch Cave for a cup of icy cold caramel goodness. Jane keeps fidgeting with the chain strap on her black metallic purse as if she's about to have a root canal.

After we order and take a seat in a booth, I ask, "Why are you acting so nervous? Is it because Chance left?"

He had to return to Little Rock for work, so he left yesterday. I believe he has it bad for Jane, so I bet he'll return soon.

"I need to tell you something." The door pings, interrupting Jane. Her eyes double in size, and she smiles.

I swivel just in time to lock eyes with my mother, Dr. Krystal Avery. She looks like she just walked out of an episode of Grey's Anatomy in her blue scrubs, white coat, and stethoscope hanging around her neck.

Her throat bobs a swallow as she steps up to our booth. "Clara Dean?"

The small lines in her forehead and slight crinkles around her eyes when she frowns are the only signs she's pushing fifty.

"Mother." My tone is crisp as my eyes dart from hers to the napkin holder.

When I look up, her lower lip trembles. "I heard you were in town."

I shift in my seat. "Yep."

"Will you be here long?" She lowers her gaze to the counter, and she also seems nervous.

What is wrong with everybody this morning?

Mom finally clamps her eyes onto mine, and tears pool on her lashes. "I'd like to spend some time with you."

I ignore her question and ask one of my own. "How's Mr. Avery?" Maybe I'm feeling hateful this morning. That could be why everyone is so fidgety.

She licks her lips and meets my glare head-on. "We're divorced. He moved to Colorado three months ago. I've been trying to call you..."

I blink rapidly. That was so unexpected. Teenage Clara would be rejoicing. Adult Clara, not so much.

Maybe because my childhood is already behind me, and what that woman does now doesn't matter. "Wow, whose idea was that? Or did another man come along that you like better?"

Jane gasps. Before she could respond, the barista yells my name. I bolt out of the booth so fast that I nearly knock Mom down on the way to the counter.

Mom exits in a hurry. I take my coffee and slide into the booth. When I work up the courage to meet Jane's gaze, her eyes are narrowed. "Clara Dean Sharp, that was the meanest thing you have ever said to your mama."

Clearly, Jane hasn't been present for all our past conversations.

Jane continues, "She was bawling her eyes out when she left. Are you happy?"

"Of course, I'm not happy. But everything that's happened is her fault." I clamp my teeth together before standing. Jane is right. What I said was hateful. "I'll be right back."

I spot Mom's convertible Lexus right away. Even though the top is up, I see her head bent over her steering wheel. Now I suddenly feel even more ashamed of what I said.

She lifts her head as I get into the car. I smooth my baby blue slacks before meeting her watery gaze. "I'm sorry for being rude."

Moisture spills from her lashes as she dabs her eyes with a tissue. "I appreciate that so much."

"Okay then, I'll see you later," I say, opening the door.

"Clara, wait."

I pause and meet her gaze, feeling my heart race as a longing I can't describe takes hold. Mom and I used to be very close, sharing everything before Mr. Avery took her away.

Once she moved out, everything changed. I wish we could regain that closeness, honestly, but I can't seem to release this intense anger inside me. She should have been there.

"I've already asked God to forgive me," Mom continues with tears flooding her face. "Will you forgive me?"

Knots coil in my stomach, and I don't know what to say. I open my mouth to say I forgive her, but the words don't come out.

Instead, I say, "How about you let me get through this first week working for Abigail, and we can spend time together next week?"

A spark of hope lights her dark eyes. "Really?"

Did she notice how I sidestepped answering her question? Maybe, but I'm fighting off a panic attack, and I just want to get out of this car.

I gulp down a steadying breath. "I can make it work if you can."

She sobs and nods her head. "I have some business in Little Rock this week, but I'll gladly cancel if you want me to."

"No, next week works better for me. Does that sound alright?" I say, glancing at her with a hint of hope in my eyes, that I quickly push away.

"Okay." She offers a timid smile, the kind that reaches her eyes and lights up her face, making me momentarily forget the weight of our past.

"See you then," I add, my voice softening as I open the door to her car, the air thick with the smell of bacon from the nearby cafe.

"I love you, Clara," she says.

My heart swells with emotion as I take a step back, unsure of how to handle the mixed feelings that overwhelm me.

"Love you, too," I reply as I close the door and watch her drive away, grinning like I just gave her the keys to my Maserati. Which I would never give to anyone. Jane hasn't even driven it.

I flip around and meet Jane's curious stare. She lifts herself off the bench and plunges toward me. "What did you say?"

"I apologized, and we agreed to meet one day next week. You happy?"

"Yes. Very." Jane's eyes brighten, and she looks pleased.

Still unsure of my feelings, I focus on counting the cars passing us by when we start the short trek to Abigail's office on the square. This normally helps when I feel anxious.

After a blue Toyota Highlander passes, I turn to Jane. "What did you want to tell me earlier?"

"I think you'll just have to see at this point." She bites her bottom lip as she opens the door to the Design Firm.

"See what?" I am so confused—until Abigail struts out of her office, with Archer Banks following behind.

His lips lift at the corners as he meets my gaze. It should be against the law for a man to look so good in crisp blue jeans and a plum V-neck popover with a white t-shirt peeking out. "Good morning, Clara and Jane."

I grab Jane by the arm and drag her out the front door. "What is he doing here?"

"Well, the thing is, um..." she scratches the back of her neck. "What do you have against Archer anyway? He apologized for calling you a cheater."

My stiff spine deflates as I realize I'm the one acting foolish. Again. Between Mom and Archer Banks, I seem to have forgotten my manners. "You know what? You're right. I don't know what my problem is."

Abigail opens the door. "Is everything okay?"

"Yes, it's fine," Jane says. "Clara is just having a hard morning. She ran into Miss Krystal."

"Oh." Abigail presses her lips together as we file

back inside the modern space. She spent many nights comforting me after Mom left us, so she knows how upsetting the situation is. "Archer, sorry about that. We're ready to get started."

"Clara? Are you ready?" His blue eyes pin me, and I can't breathe. I can't think, so I nod.

Abigail smiles. "Archer, as CEO of Lombardi Enterprises, I want to express how much we appreciate your trust in our firm."

CEO? My heart kicks into high gear, and I think I may faint.

Trevor works for Archer Banks. That must be why he thought we were still engaged.

Not sure why Trevor wouldn't have told him we broke up, but I know firsthand he's a liar. And why had Trevor not told me? He knows I am a huge football fan.

Archer's smile grabs my attention, dazzling all three of us, but he keeps his eyes on me. "Abigail, I'm looking forward to working with your team. As CEO, I plan to be very hands-on with this project."

My knees turn to pudding. And for some reason, I have a feeling fainting right now is the least of my worries.

Chapter 14

Archer

The look on Clara's face is priceless as we discuss not only a new office in downtown Mountain View but also a redesign of a two-story log cabin I'm interested in purchasing.

This morning's style is a cream-colored blouse, baby blue slacks with white strappy heels, I have no doubt I'd break my neck in. A far cry from the oversized sweatshirts, button-ups, and jeans I'm used to seeing her in.

She could go up against any businesswoman in a

fashion contest and win. A fashion contest? When did I start caring about fashion? I'm wearing a purple-looking shirt, the t-shirt I slept in, and basic jeans.

My heart is acutely aware of her presence as she twists a chocolate brown curl cascading past her shoulders around her finger. She nibbles on her full bottom lip, and my mind wanders to how she felt in my arms when we fell in the stream. My mouth goes dry. I swallow a sip of water and force my thoughts to the present.

Unaware of how my mind is racing, Abigail gets down to business. "From what I understand, you want a cozy office to house four employees. I believe we'll find the perfect space." She glances at her iPad. "I have several ideas we can run by you."

"That's great," I say, resting my arm on the plush, white sofa. "I also have another project I'd like to discuss."

"What's that?"

"I came across an older two-story log cabin while exploring. It could be a solid investment for an Inn or Bed and Breakfast, and I'm considering purchasing the property." The initial plan was to get an office running before we scout locations for rentals, but the cabin is perfect.

"I'd love to see it."

Jane scoots to the edge of her seat. "Me, too. Is it old?"

"It appears to have been built in the 1950s, possibly earlier. I'll call Sid and see if he can show it to us this afternoon. Will that work?" Sid Blackstone is the realtor I've been working with and an all-around nice guy.

"Yes. I've cleared my schedule for the day."

I step away to make the call, and he lets me know he can meet any time. "My realtor is free now. I let him know we could be there in twenty minutes."

"Sounds perfect."

On the way to the cabin, I swivel in the front seat and glance at Clara, sitting in the back seat behind Abigail. She remains quiet, seemingly engrossed in the scenery. I don't blame her. Trees litter the mountainside as they zip by through the window.

"Archer, I'm excited to see this cabin," Abigail says, breaking the silence. "The drive is a good one, and I think people would love to stay in this area, especially since it's close to Blanchard Springs."

"I agree," I say with a nod, before we fall back into

a comfortable silence for a few miles.

When we arrive, Sid is already at the cabin. I say hello as my eyes drink in the spectacular scenery. Perched atop a mountain, it offers a breathtaking view filled with shimmering water, rolling hills, and lush trees.

Clara's hand goes to her throat as she stops beside me, her gaze on the cabin. "This is breathtaking."

A vanilla fragrance washes over me that I recognize as distinctly Clara's.

There's no way I'm not buying this cabin.

Chapter 15

Clara

It's Friday night, and all I want is a cup of Raspberry Coffee from Sasquatch Cave and to relax.

After spending the week going from space to space with Abigail and Jane, I'm exhausted.

Who knew trying to find the perfect Lombardi Enterprises office could be so tiring?

At least Archer spent most of the week in Little Rock.

Jane is out with Chance, so I'm heading out solo.

As I brush my teeth, music drifts through the open

bathroom window.

I glance outside. Two groups of people are jamming in the lot across the street under gazebos.

My phone pings with a text from Donny.

He must be bored.

DONNY

Hey, sis. What you doing?

CLARA

Watching a jam session at the park. Thinking about freeing Mr. Bingley

DONNY

DO IT! And send a video

CLARA

I might. But no video.

DONNY

Loser

CLARA

You'll never believe who I met.

DONNY

Wanna give me a hint?

My phone buzzes with an incoming FaceTime, and as soon as I pick up, Donny dives right in. "Lies!"

"I'm telling the truth! His dad is actually dating Abigail," I reply, trying to keep a smile off my face.

"I don't believe you. You're a good liar. You made me think Dad adopted me. Remember?"

"That's not fair! I was like twelve when I told you Johnny Cash was your biological father."

"You were fourteen. I still remember getting laughed at when I gave a presentation to my fifth-grade class about my famous father," he says, shaking his head.

The last summer we had as a family, Mom and Dad took us to Dyess, Arkansas, and we toured Johnny Cash's boyhood home. I got the idea to tell Donny that he was Johnny Cash's kid when he kept playing his music after we left. "Sorry, but I still take credit for your love of music."

He chuckles. "I believed I was named after Johnny instead of our grandfather for the longest. But you're right, that did spark my love of music. I figured if I was Johnny Cash's kid, then I should be a good musician."

I do my best to keep from laughing. "You know I've apologized a million times already! I was kidding and didn't realize you believed me."

"I know that. But I'm still gonna need proof that you've met Archer Banks."

"Fine, I'll send pictures."

"Good. I'll pretend I believe you for now. Did you confess your love?"

"No!"

"Did you at least get him to sign your jersey?"

"Nope. I can't handle this line of questioning right now. I've got to run, you goof. Love you!"

"Love you too, sis. I'll be waiting for pictures. And I'll know if they're AI."

I hang up and glance at my fiddle. Like in Pride and Prejudice, my Mr. Bingley was always well regarded until conflict entered the picture. I guess I was like Mrs. Bennett, who outwardly said she wanted nothing to do with him after he slighted her daughter, but inwardly she hoped to see more of him. That is so me right now. "I know it's been a while, but my music left me, buddy. I'm sorry."

Now I'm talking to my fiddle. I take another long glance at the scene below, pick up my case and jog down the stairs.

A young woman looks at my case and smiles. "You play?"

I shrug. "A little."

"Then what are you waiting for?" She grabs my hand and leads me to the group.

Are all eyes on me, or am I imagining things? I glance at the ground and take a deep breath before I remove Mr. Bingley from his prison.

After ensuring my wrist is straight and my chin is not at an awkward angle, I place my fingers on the strings and hold the bow. Mama used to tell me to have fun and not stress when I play. Now would be a good time to take her advice.

My arms move of their own accord, and the music coming from Mr. Bingley is sweet to my ears. After a few minutes, I lose myself to the music and stomp my feet along to the beat. When the song ends, I put Mr. Bingley in his case and slip away.

My entire body buzzes with excitement. That is, until I come around the ice cream parlor and narrowly escape colliding with Archer Banks, who's leaning against the side of the little building.

Chapter 16

Clara

My breath hitches as I meet Archer's gaze. His smile and the twinkle in his exotic eyes catch me off guard, and my knees give out.

If possible, his grin doubles in size as he reaches out to steady me. "I'm beginning to think you keep running into me on purpose."

My hand grips the case as heat covers my neck. "I do not. What are you doing here anyway?"

He points across the street. "We're staying at the inn."

Of course, he is. I mean, I can't blame him for staying at The Inn at Mountain View. It's so homey and comfortable, I'd be there too if my stay was shorter.

After a thirty-second stare-off, he raises a brow. "Can we start over?" he asks and looks my way as if trying to gauge my reaction.

"What do you mean?" I don't know why I'm playing dumb. It's obvious he's referring to my attitude.

"I mean, will you accept my apology for how I acted on the blind date?" He asks, searching my face.

Why does he have to be so adorable and look so sincere?

I bite my bottom lip and try to wrap my head around the fact that Archer Banks is looking at me like I'm his favorite person in the world right now.

And I *like* it.

"Fine. I accept your apology."

"Good." His adorable dimples suddenly appear, making him even more attractive, if that is even possible. "Wanna go grab a coffee?"

Yes, sir. On the way there, we should stop by the preacher's house. "Um, I guess I could drink a coffee. Let me put my things away first."

What's wrong with me? I do not want to marry

Archer Banks. Not at all.

Sure, I've dreamed of our first kiss for three years, but that was before I met him in person.

A little later, Archer, still oblivious to the fact that I was planning our wedding, and I plop down on a bench, each of us with a coffee from Sasquatch Cave.

He takes a sip of his and glances in my direction. "How do you think Chance and Jane are doing on their date?"

I take my phone out and tap Jane's name before turning it in his direction. A picture of Jane and Chance grinning from ear to ear takes up the screen.

Archer leans close enough that I can feel the heat from his coffee on my cheek as he smiles at the photo Jane sent me.

"Looks like they're having a good time."

"Yep." I barely squeak out as I slip my phone into my bag. He's sitting way too close.

He turns his head, and our faces are mere centimeters apart. He drops his gaze to my lips.

My heart thumps.

Hard.

Can this really be happening? Is he going to kiss me? It looks like he's going to, as he sways closer. I have never in my life let someone kiss me on a first date. Well, unless you count the boy at the Ozark Folk Center kissing my cheek when I was a kid, but no one since then.

And this is definitely not a date. But am I seriously going to let Archer Banks kiss me?

Yes, stupid. How many times have I planned this exact moment in my mind?

Wait. Didn't I decide earlier that we would never work out?

Regardless of any hasty decisions I may or may not have made earlier, I close my eyes and keep my face turned toward him, waiting for the kiss that will change my life.

It doesn't come.

When I open my eyes, Archer's gaze is pointed at the ground.

Embarrassment floods my body. How could I have misread things so badly?

The real question is, in what alternate reality would Archer Banks ever kiss me? I need my head checked. There will be no kissing.

Not now.

Not ever.

After watching my dad try to hide his heartbreak for so many years and then my own with Trevor, I don't even want to start anything with Archer. How can I trust him with my heart?

I spring to my feet. Hot coffee sloshes onto my arm, soaking my shirt sleeve. "Thanks for the coffee," I say, ignoring my burning arm.

His brow furrows as his gaze falls to my wet shirt. "Are you okay?"

"Sure. I'm fine." I wave with a big smile to prove my point before I take off toward my apartment.

Archer stands. "I'm sorry if I hurt your feelings..."

He says something else I can't quite make out as I continue zipping toward the music store and my escape.

It took Trevor three dates to get a kiss. Three. What happened to Clara Dean Banks that she'd allow someone she isn't even dating to kiss her?

And the worst part? He didn't want to kiss me. I totally misread things.

I know I've said it before, but I'm confident this will be the last time I see Archer Banks for anything other than work.

And I didn't even get a picture for Donny.

Chapter 17

Archer

E ven though the cool May morning has zero humidity, sweat pours down my face as I run through the wooded area, half listening to Chance. He's told me about his past few dates with Jane three times now.

But all I can think about is how Clara looked playing her fiddle last night. If I thought she had filled my dreams before, she dominated them after seeing that performance. Not to mention the almost kiss. I am such a loser. She wanted to kiss me, and I blew it. She probably hates me.

Chance darts past me. "I like her."

"I'm glad you like her. I just hope she doesn't hold it against you when her mom and my dad break things off."

We head up an incline, and I pass Chance. He catches up. "What makes you think they're going to break things off? I think they're good."

I know my dad, and he's never dated a woman for more than a few months since we lost Mom. His relationship with Abigail will be no different.

"Yeah, but he doesn't know how to commit. They'll break up sooner or later."

His forehead creases. "I disagree. Have you noticed the way he looks at Abigail?"

No, and I don't want to. I stop running to take a swig from my water bottle. "Not particularly. Like I said, it'll end, so why even attempt to form an attachment?"

"You sound like a CEO, dude." He makes a face and uses quotations before mocking me in his best British aristocratic accent. "I apologize for my rudeness, but I don't want to form an attachment."

"You're not funny." Okay, he's funny, but I can't let

him know I think so.

"Liar," he shoots back, a smirk playing at the corners of his lips.

"I'm not a liar," I insist, trying to sound more convincing than I feel.

His gaze turns eagle-eyed, and he leans in slightly. "Your jaw is ticking, so you *are* lying about me not being funny."

I roll my eyes and change the subject. "Well, I almost kissed Clara last night."

He slaps me lightly in the chest like he's shocked. "How did that happen?"

I take a deep breath, and Clara's green eyes and the way she leaned in for a kiss cross my mind. "I ran into her, and we went for a coffee." For some reason, I don't tell him about her fiddle playing. I want to keep that tidbit of information to myself.

His brows furrow, and I can see his mind working. "No, but seriously, how did you go from thinking she's a cheater to almost kissing her this past week?"

"It was no big deal. I think I got caught up in the moment," I reply, trying to downplay the whirlwind of emotions invading my space.

"What moment?" Chance presses, his lips edging

up at the corners.

My phone buzzes, interrupting the start of an interrogation. I raise a brow as Trevor's name flashes across my screen. I answer and put the phone on speaker. "Hey, Trevor. What can I do for you?"

"Morning, boss. I wanted to tell you I found a possible deal on a boutique hotel in Kansas City."

"Okay. Shoot me an email with details."

"Will do," he replies, a hint of relief in his tone. "How are things in Mountain View?"

"Fine. I ran into your fiancée the other day." For some reason, I can't wait to hear what he says.

Trevor coughs a nervous sound. "I've been meaning to talk to you about that."

"Why did you tell me the wedding planning was going well?"

"Honestly, I was embarrassed."

"Embarrassed about what?"

"Clara ended our engagement a few months ago."

"Okay. Things like that happen all the time. But why lie about it?"

"Can I just apologize and say it's a long story?"

"We'll talk when I get back to the city." My tone is firm as I hang up the phone, cutting off any chance for him to respond. I'm not one to be lied to. If he'd lie about that, what else is he keeping from me?

My mind goes back to the day I met Clara at the office, and I can't help but wonder if that's the day she ended things. She did seem on edge, and there were tears in her eyes. I assumed it was because she twisted her ankle, but now I would bet that's the day things went south for Trevor and Clara. And what about the red lipstick on Trevor? Clara wasn't wearing lipstick that day. Why have I not thought about this before now?

Guilt for how I treated her at the restaurant weighs heavily on me. I tell Chance how Clara and I first met as we make our way to my Hummer. Even though I'm having a normal conversation with Chance, my mind is on Clara and what I can do to make up for how I treated her. Chance's mouth forms an O as it hangs open. "I knew Trevor was trouble."

My life is too busy for a relationship, but I can at least show her that I'm not the jerk she probably thinks I am. This morning will be a perfect time to start since we have a meeting to discuss the project.

Later on, Clara stops in front of me while Abigail and Jane go inside AB Design. "I'll talk to Abigail about hiring another freelance designer. I don't want things to be awkward for you."

"No, I want you." I hear myself say.

Her face brightens, and she smiles a genuine smile that reaches her eyes. "Really? You've seen my designs?"

"Can't say that I have," I say, wondering if she's aware how looking into her eyes can cause grown men to forget their names.

"Then how do you know you want me on the project?" The moment she rakes her teeth over her bottom lip, I know I'm a goner.

"I have a feeling you and I would be good together." How can a woman I barely know capture my attention like this?

She meets my gaze momentarily before turning her attention to a black mustang with a loud motor passing by. "Hmmm. Okay."

"About last night –" I begin, but she cuts me off.

"Let's just forget it. You know, I was ready to… never mind."

"Yes, I know." I long to close the distance between us. But we're not alone, so that's out of the question. "I didn't want our first kiss to happen while you were still unsure whether you liked me."

Surprise flickers in her eyes. "Oh really?"

"Yes, really." I wonder what she'd think if she knew how I discussed with Dad and Abigail whether Clara and I spending time together would be a conflict of interest. I explained how Jane tried to fix us up, and they both told me to go for it. Apparently, Clara is not a full-time employee, so what we do in our free time is our own business.

"You think we'll have a first kiss, huh? Feeling a bit cocky, are we?" Clara gives me a teasing smile.

I can barely contain the grin spreading across my face. Even so, I shrug, trying to play it cool. "Maybe I should've warned you about my charm," I reply with a playful wink.

Clara narrows her eyes, clearly not convinced. "You better not be a serial killer, you know."

I chuckle. "I told you to ask the security guard that day, remember? If you didn't follow the instructions, that's on you, not me."

"Well, I'll have you know that my cousin finds killers for a living," she shoots back, crossing her arms defiantly.

I raise an eyebrow, intrigued. "Oh really? And who might that be?"

"Tammy Sharp," she replies, her tone a mix of pride and seriousness.

"From Pocahontas?" I ask, recognition dawning on me.

"Yeah, you know her?" Clara's expression shifts to one of curiosity.

"Oh no, Betsy told me all about her," I say, referring to Betsy, my grandfather's dedicated nursing aide, who has an uncanny knack for gossiping about the most fascinating people.

"Betsy?" Clara questions, tilting her head.

"Yeah, my grandfather's nursing aide is quite the character," I say, chuckling. Noticing the confusion on her face, I add, "Betsy has become like an aunt to me, and she's into true crime. She's always sharing stories about local news and murders in Arkansas."

Clara's smile sends a warm flutter through me, even making my knuckles tingle. I've never experienced such strong emotions before, and honestly, I'm not sure how I feel about it.

Chapter 18

Clara

Jane sprawls next to me on her mom's antique sofa, which totally reminds me of the one from the Bennetts' house when Mr. Bingley and Mr. Darcy showed up out of nowhere.

Every time I see it, I can't help but picture the Bennett ladies running around the room, speed cleaning before Darcy and Bingley got to the door.

I wouldn't be surprised if Abigail had it shipped over from the United Kingdom, directly from the set of Pride and Prejudice.

"Archer hasn't been too much to deal with, has he?" Jane asks.

"No, he's been nice ever since he apologized." Heat floods my cheeks as I think about the almost kiss.

"Why are you turning red?" She narrows her eyes, giving me her full attention.

"I may have tried to kiss Archer, but we weren't on the same page." Tears brim at my eyelids.

A flash of anger crosses Jane's face. "That stupid jerk. I really am sorry I didn't tell you he was here."

"I get the feeling he likes me, but I don't know if things could ever work out between us. Can we just not talk about him right now? I want to watch Pride and Prejudice," I say, jutting my lip out.

"Okay," she replies, pulling the remote out from behind a pillow before handing it to me. "We can watch it."

"Yes!" I waste no time pulling up Jane's Netflix account.

Before the movie starts, Jane leans her chin in her hand and looks at me with a mixture of concern and curiosity. "I was beginning to wonder if something was seriously wrong with you."

I feel the crease between my eyes deepening. "What

do you mean?"

She shoots me a knowing look. "How long have you dreamed about meeting and falling in love with your precious football player, Archer Banks?"

"Hush!" I whisper as I scan the area to make sure no one else hears her. "He's not what I was expecting, okay?"

She folds her arms across her chest. "Are you sure he didn't want to kiss you?"

"Yes, I'm positive." I bang my head on the couch and immediately regret it. It's not the softest in the world. "You're right, though, you really should've told me he was here."

"For the millionth time, I'm sorry." She sits up and pulls the neon yellow scrunchie out of her hair. "I thought it was a good idea at the time."

"I know you did, and it's fine-ish. I guess things just got off on the wrong foot with us. But things –"

The front door swings open just as I was about to tell Jane about the conversation Archer and I had this morning.

The man on my mind strides in with his dad and Chance behind him. They're all carrying bags.

He smiles at me, his eyes crinkling. "We're grilling

burgers and hot dogs. I hope you're hungry."

"Always," I say as my stomach flip-flops.

Jane waits until they're on the back patio before she turns to me. "I feel like something happened between y'all this morning. Am I right?"

My mind goes back to Archer talking about our first kiss, and I debate whether I should tell her. I know I *will* tell her, but right now may not be the best time for her to scream and act like a fool since Archer and his dad are out back grilling burgers and hot dogs.

Who knew CEO's grilled basic stuff like hot dogs? For some reason, it makes Archer seem more attainable.

"I'll tell you all the details later," I say as I stare at Archer through the sliding glass door, laughing at something his dad said.

A few minutes later, Abigail walks through the front door with a huge smile. "Look who I ran into at the nursing home."

My gramma files in behind Abigail, giving off Rose from the Golden Girls vibes. Oh, my goodness, she's a looker even at sixty-five. "Gramma!" I run across the room and wrap her in a hug. "What are you doing here?"

"I came to see an old friend who's in the nursing home. Abigail was there visiting the residents and invited me over."

"I'm so happy to see you," I say before kissing her cheek.

"Hi, there," Gramma says, her gaze traveling to the back door as Archer steps inside, wearing white Nike shorts and a Sasquatch Cave t-shirt.

Archer grins as he meets her gaze. "Hello," he says, stopping in front of Gramma. "I'm Archer Banks."

"Call me Gramma. And I know who you are well enough, young man." Gramma says as she glances at me, making my heart nearly fall out of my chest. "Even without your beard."

He rubs his cleanly shaven face. "Most people don't recognize me without it."

"You're handsome either way," Gramma says, nodding in my direction with a smile that reminds me of the cat Azrael from the Smurfs cartoon, when it's about to eat Papa Smurf. "Just ask my Clara Dean."

Please don't say anything. Please don't say anything.

She points her thumb in my direction, and I know she *will* say it. "This one here once dragged me to

Vegas to watch you play ball."

She said it.

The smile on Archer's face is mesmerizing.

Why do I have the urge to kiss his dimples?

Because Jane is right. Something is seriously wrong with me. It must be.

"You came to Vegas for one of my games?" Archer asks, his grin seeming to double in size.

"I wanted to go shopping and figured I could do both." Technically, that is not a lie. I did want to go shopping. I wanted to visit a cute little shopping mall in Vegas.

Gramma, who will be known as Azrael at least the rest of the day, must disagree. She puts her hand on her hip and tsks. "Now that's one of the biggest lies you've ever told."

"Gramma!"

"What?"

Thank goodness Paul chooses that moment to poke his head inside. "Burgers and hot dogs are ready."

Abigail rushes past Gramma. I'd think she was hiding a laugh if I didn't know better. She clears her throat. "Good, I'm famished."

We head to the back patio, where Abigail has seating

for ten and has turned the area into an outdoor paradise. String lights surround the wood awning, and flowers and climbing vines surround a water fountain.

Archer pulls a chair out and smiles at Gramma. She sits and glances at me with a smug smile. "This young man has manners, Clara Dean."

Archer claims the chair next to hers and also looks at me with a smug smile.

After blessing the food, Paul gazes at Abigail. "I think we should tell the story of how we met."

She giggles and looks at me. "Not to bring up a bad memory for Clara, but I went to Little Rock to give her ex a piece of my mind."

I take a sip of water and eyeball Abigail.

Paul continues their story, "I saw her giving one of the security guards a hard time about not telling her where Trevor was, so I stopped and asked if I could help with anything."

"I told him I was there to see you know who, and I told him why." Abigail's brow creases. "I was ready to knock some sense into him."

Paul meets Abigail's gaze. "I suggested she go to lunch with me instead. And we've been staying in touch via phone until a few weeks ago."

Jane narrows her eyes. "You went to lunch with a complete stranger?"

Paul laughs. "The security guard vouched for me."

Archer nudges my leg under the table and points back and forth between us. "See, Clara Dean, this could've all been avoided had you asked the security guard about me that day."

Normally, only Gramma and Mom call me Clara Dean. It's not a bad name, but I prefer Clara. However, the way Archer says it has my heart racing. It feels so intimate coming from his lips.

"What are you talking about?" Gramma asks, breaking the spell, I've found myself under.

Archer proceeds to tell the story of the day we met.

Gramma shakes her head. "How did you not recognize Archer Banks? You swooned over him enough, you should've known his face, even without the beard."

Heat travels up my neck, and I consider crawling under the table. "In my defense, I thought he looked like Archer, but I had no reason to think he'd be in Little Rock, Arkansas, working at or even visiting Lombardi Enterprises."

Jane looks at me across the table. "Clara, did I tell

you I saw our old friend Lisa the other day?"

I love how she smoothly changes the subject, and I make a mental note to bring her coffee in the morning. "Yeah, you mentioned that."

A few minutes later, Paul clears his throat. "Archer and I have a last-minute board meeting in Little Rock this week."

The rest of the conversation fades away as I consider not seeing Archer for a while. Part of me wants to jump for joy, because I know I should squash these feelings I'm catching.

He's moving on soon, and I don't do summer flings.

No, thank you.

My goal: forget about Archer Banks.

Then why do I already feel his absence?

After I finish my burger, I take my plate to the kitchen so I can breathe without feeling watched. I rub my arms as I walk to the open window. A bird feeder hanging from a wooden post sways in the breeze, and I imagine myself like a bird, fluttering from one place to another.

It's time for me to choose somewhere to live and plant roots. Could I be happy in Mountain View?

What about Mom? Is it possible for us to move past the years of hurt?

If I'm honest with myself, I'd admit that I want her back in my life. I need my mom, but how can I let go of this ball of fury I've carried around since high school?

Tears burn the back of my throat. Gritting my teeth, I swallow them down. I want a place to call home. That's the missing piece in my life.

The woodsy scent that makes me want to bury my face in Archer's neck greets me as he stops beside me. He nudges his shoulder into mine. "What are you thinking about?"

"Happiness," I say softly.

He tilts his head and meets my gaze, as if he's peering into my soul. "Are you thinking about you being happy or happiness in general?"

"Maybe," I reply with a shrug, doing my best to ignore the soothing, warm hum his presence stirs in me. "Just contemplating happiness overall."

His piercing gaze holds me captive. "I would like to make you happy, Clara."

My cheeks flush so intensely I feel like I could set this house ablaze. I look down, and for some reason, I still feel moisture brushing my lids.

Archer must notice, because in a split second, his arms wrap around me, pulling me close. I melt into his body, accepting the comfort he offers.

He presses a kiss to the side of my head, and I freeze. My feelings for this football player go far beyond just a crush. Standing here together, I can't shake the feeling that Archer is the home I so desperately want and need.

Chapter 19

Clara

Archer made an offer on the cabin on Monday, which was accepted the same day. I can't believe how excited I am to work on this design. This is not only my first major project, but it's also for Archer Banks.

My life right now: I have finally met my favorite football player! On top of that, he has been flirting with me. But is he just toying with me? I can't help but think a relationship with Archer is in the realm of impossible. It's unreal, almost like a fourteen-year-old

Clara meeting and dating Harry Styles.

I lean back into the hot pink office chair and grin at Jane. "I can't believe Abigail is giving us the cabin design."

"Right? I think she just wants more time with Paul." She smirks before sticking her tongue out.

I giggle. "They're so cute together."

"Yeah, I guess. I just want her to be happy."

Jane has never met her father. She's not even sure if he's alive or what his name is since he and Abigail got together in college, and he left before finding out she was pregnant.

We drop the subject when Archer enters the front door with Paul and Abigail lagging behind.

She beams when Paul grasps her hand. "We settled on an office space."

"It's ideal for what we're going for." Archer walks to the water fountain and downs a cup in one drink.

Paul's lips lift into a smile. "We also stopped by Urban Forge. That place has the most unique and well-made furniture I've seen."

"Yes, I plan to purchase everything for the cabin there," Archer says.

Abigail grinned at Archer. "Yes, I think ordering

custom pieces is the way to go for your cabin. Especially with you planning on making it a vacation destination property."

Archer meets Paul's gaze, looking excited. "I agree."

"That's great news." Jane glances at Paul's and Abigail's hands.

"I plan to clean out the cabin today," Abigail states just as her phone starts ringing. "I have to take this," she adds, moving to the back of the room.

After a minute or so, she returns, looking flustered. "That was Ray. Shawna is missing."

Jane gasps. "What?"

"He and Olivia are beside themselves. They think she snuck out in the middle of the night."

Jane rises from her seat. "Oh no."

"Her bed hadn't been slept in this morning. She went to her room around ten last night, and that's the last time they saw her."

"Have they called her friends?" I ask.

"I'm sure they have. Jane, honey, we need to go to Oklahoma, " she says before glancing at me. "I'm sorry. Clara, will you please take the lead here? We'll touch base as soon as possible."

"Absolutely," I say before hugging Abigail and then

Jane. "I'll get a jump on decluttering and cleaning out the cabin."

"I'll be here the rest of the week as well." Archer nods in my direction. "Clara and I will tag team whatever needs to be done."

Abigail squeezes Archer's hand. "I appreciate you."

"I'm going with you," Paul says. "That is, if you want me to."

Abigail smiles at Paul. "Of course. I could use your support. I just need to book our flights."

"No need." Paul holds up a hand. "We can take the company plane." He looks at Archer, who nods in agreement. Paul continues, "Where in Oklahoma does your brother live? I'll make the arrangements."

A little later, Archer and I make eye contact when the door closes behind Jane. "Long story short, Shawna is Abigail's niece. She keeps running off."

"Oh. How old is she?"

"Twenty, but she's autistic."

"I hope they find her."

"Me, too. Thank you for letting them take the plane."

His neck reddens. I cock my head and study his profile. I can't believe Archer is embarrassed over owning a plane.

He shrugs. "It's no big deal. Are you ready to go to the cabin?"

"Sure." My stomach pitches with the thought of being alone with Archer. It's just a job I keep repeating in my head.

Then why am I so nervous?

Chapter 20

Archer

Let me make one thing clear: I am not happy a girl is missing, and I pray they find her safe and sound.

One thing I am genuinely happy about? Clara, with her bright smile and tousled hair, sitting in the front seat of my Hummer, nibbling on a Caramello bar. The way she concentrates on keeping the gooey caramel from dripping down her chin is utterly adorable.

Yet, it's not just the sight of her struggle with the

candy bar that brings a smile to my face; the simple fact she is in the vehicle with me makes me smile like a fool.

What is wrong with me? Before I can figure it out, a call comes in from my football coach. Clara's eyes widen when she sees his name on the screen.

I tap to answer. "Hey, Coach."

"Archer! How are things in Arkansas?"

"Going good. How are you?"

"I'll be honest, I was hoping you'd say you hate it there."

Clara stares at the glowing screen, her chocolate bar long forgotten as the chocolate melts on her fingers. The intensity in her gaze reveals a passion for football I might have underestimated.

"I don't hate it, that's for sure." I keep my tone light, trying not to give away the fact I have a huge crush.

"You dating somebody?" I can hear the smirk in his voice. Clearly, I failed at keeping my tone light.

"Not yet, " I say, as my gaze bounces over to Clara.

He chuckles. "You sound happy."

"I am," I admit, a smile creeping on my face as I risk a quick glance at Clara. We are not dating; that's for sure, but I like spending time with her. That's all.

Nothing serious happening here.

"There's no chance I can talk you into coming back?"

"Sorry, sir, but family comes first." I want to say yes so badly I can't stand it. But right now, Dad is not up to being the CEO. Someday? Maybe.

"I thought you'd say that, but I had to ask."

After a few minutes of light banter, we end the call. I smile at Clara, who is still staring at the screen, oblivious to the melted chocolate that's now on her jean shorts. "So, just how big of a football fan are you?"

A faint grin crosses her face. "I don't know what you're talking about."

"I think you're lying." I tease, raising my eyebrow.

"Maybe," she says, a playful smirk betraying her earlier denial.

I file this information away for later. Maybe I can take her to meet the team someday. I blink a few times as the realization hits me: I'm making future plans with Clara Sharp, and she doesn't even know it.

I pull into the driveway and take in the view. "Want to explore the area before we start on the cabin?"

"Sure."

After a few minutes of walking in silence, she looks

up and meets my gaze, a hint of vulnerability in her eyes. "I have to admit the truth to you."

I swallow and run my hand through my hair, my mind going straight to Trevor. If she tells me they're getting back together, I might scream. "Okay."

"I love football, and Coach Duncan is a silver fox."

Laughter pours from me. "A silver fox?" I can't wait to tell him what she said.

"I mean, yeah." Her teasing grin is almost my undoing. "He is."

My gaze drops to her lips before I quickly drag my eyes to the stream running along the property. "This stream is nice." *This stream is nice?* How have I managed to forget how to have a normal conversation with a beautiful woman?

"Yes, it is. I think it adds a lot of value to the property." We walk back toward the cabin, and she points around the yard. "I envision a gazebo with fairy lights over there, surrounded by an enchanted garden." She continues talking about the yard and how it could draw people in, but I can only think about how perfect she is.

We linger outside for a few more minutes, taking in the serenity of the property before I finally unlock the door, and we step into the dimly lit interior.

A rustling sound erupts from behind a dusty box piled high in one corner, causing my heart to race. Clara's fingers tighten around my forearm as I grab a walking stick from beside the front door. I put a finger to my lip, signaling for her to be quiet as I tiptoe toward the sound, Clara right behind me.

The box moves.

A gasp escapes my lips when we come face to face with an unexpected visitor: a skunk, its black body contrasted by the stark white stripes running down its back.

Clara lets out a high-pitched shriek that echoes throughout the cabin. The skunk, sensing the commotion, raises its fluffy tail high in the air as a clear warning right before it sprays us.

A horrific scent fills the air, dousing our clothes and making my stomach churn as we scramble to escape the intruder.

Chapter 21

Clara

I stink. Even after three scalding baths soaking in hydrogen peroxide, baking soda, baby shampoo, vinegar, and every other home remedy Gramma could remember, I still smell like rotten eggs, garlic, and burnt rubber.

Now Archer and I are back at the cabin, dealing with a rogue skunk. Or at least Maegan from animal services is.

Maegan lands a grin on us. I can tell she wants to laugh, and I can even admit it's kinda funny. "It's all clear. I'll make sure the skunk is released in a safe environment."

"Far away from here, please," Archer says, pinching the bridge of his nose.

"For sure," Maegan replies with a smile she's attempting to hide before driving away.

Archer links his eyes to mine, and we stand on the front porch for a minute, just looking at one another.

I crack a grin right before laughter explodes from us both. He puts his arm around my shoulder, and my heart kicks up a notch or fifteen.

I take a few faltering steps back, only stopping when my shoulder hits the side of the cabin. "If you can stand the smell, we should get to work," I say, making a sour face.

"I'll grab the supplies."

I go inside and start opening the windows and every door. We need to air out the place.

Archer sets a bottle of vinegar and a box of bowls on the kitchen counter. "I hope this works to air out the cabin. I still stink a bit even after soaking in, I don't even know what."

"I think it will, but it'll take a while," I reply as I fight with a stubborn window that's stuck.

He stops beside me and grabs the bottom of the window. "Here, let me help you."

"I never thought I'd say this to you, but man, you stink."

His mouth falls open. "You don't exactly smell like a bed of roses."

My mouth twitches. Why am I wanting to laugh again? Getting sprayed by a skunk is no laughing matter. Archer must think it is, because he snorts a laugh.

When our amusement dies down, he raises the window and faces me, standing still. His penetrating, icy blue gaze probes my face.

My heart thuds in my chest, and I'm unable to break eye contact.

He brushes a lock of hair behind my ear before bringing his mouth so very close to mine.

I draw in a stuttered gasp as my mind turns to mush.

My phone buzzes from my back pocket, breaking the spell.

It's a text from Jane.

JANE

Shawna is safe!!!

I show Archer the screen before I answer.

CLARA

Yay! Where was she?

JANE

Girl, she was hiding in the basement.

CLARA

What? Wow

JANE

I'll tell you the rest when we get home

CLARA

Sounds good

JANE

We plan to come home tomorrow

CLARA

Safe travels. Love you

JANE

Love you.

Dots appear on the screen letting me know Jane is typing again.

Have you and Archer kissed yet?

My face burns as hot as Destin, Florida, on the fourth of July as I jerk the screen away from Archer's view.

He attempts to grab the phone from my hand. "What did that text say?"

"Nothing," I say, my cheeks blazing hot as I slip the phone into my back pocket. I ignore the incoming text. I know it's Jane, and there's no telling what she said.

Archer chuckles before he starts pouring vinegar into bowls. "I thought I saw something about us kissing on the screen."

He's smiling again, and even though my lips twitch, I don't reply. Instead, I grab a bowl and set it on a table that was left behind in the living area.

After we litter the cabin with what feels like a thousand bowls of vinegar, we climb into Archer's Hummer. "I think we should be able to come back later today," I say.

"How about we go somewhere our smell won't offend people?"

"Ha, okay. Where?"

"You up for a picnic?"

Here comes the familiar banging of my heart. I really need to learn how to control these kinds of things. "I could eat."

He opens the door and steps out. "Follow me."

"Where are we going?" I ask as I jog to keep up with his long strides.

He slips on a pair of sunglasses as he waits for me. "Just down by the stream."

I wonder where the food is as we walk, but I keep my curiosity to myself. Once we arrive at the stream, I glance around. A charming picnic basket rests on a red checkered blanket atop lush grass near the stream. "How did you manage to pull this off?"

"I made a quick call while getting the cleaning supplies," he replies with a shrug. I think I detect a hint of nervousness in his voice, but I have to be imagining things.

"Wasn't that an hour ago?" I stare at the scene in disbelief.

"Yes, but that's plenty of time."

As Archer begins to unpack several sandwiches,

fruits, and chocolate treats from the basket, my mind races with the thought that maybe, just maybe, there may be a chance for something more than friendship to spark between us after all.

Chapter 22

Archer

A strong breeze blows across the stream, sending a musky earth scent into the air. I breathe it in, feeling lighter than I have in a long time.

"Which do you prefer: quarterback or CEO?" Clara asks after swallowing the last bite of a ham and cheese sandwich.

A squirrel darts from one tree to another, stopping to study us a moment before scrambling up the tree.

The picnic has been great, and we're now playing Twenty Questions. At least that's how it feels, but I don't mind. "That's a hard one. Ask something easier."

"Favorite color?"

I tap my chin and look into her eyes. "Green."

"Lime green or forest green?"

"Green like your eyes."

She swallows and looks at the squirrel, who has made its way down the tree again.

I lean back on one elbow. "It's my turn. What's your favorite color?"

"Teal."

I file that information away and wait for her next question.

"Why did you cut your hair and shave your beard?"

After making eye contact with a turtle that crawled onto a piece of wood sticking out of the stream, I sigh. "Honestly? To keep people from recognizing me so easily."

"That makes sense. I thought you looked familiar the day we met and even considered you to resemble Archer Banks, but I was a little upset that day."

I nod. "I understand."

"Beach or mountains?" she asks, obviously changing the subject.

"Normally, I'd say beach, but these mountains have brought a lot of happiness these past few days." I sit up and take a swig of water.

Her eyes sparkle. "I bet. I'd be happy, too, with that cabin."

"I wasn't talking just about the cabin." I look at her pointedly.

A small smile brightens her face, and she blushes. "Hiking or swimming?"

"Hiking. But you skipped me." I lean across the blanket, lightly running my fingers over her bare foot. "Do you like me better as a football player or CEO?"

She curls her legs beneath her, and now I have nothing for my hands to do, so I pick up a plastic fork, flipping it around in my hand.

"What kind of question is that? I'll go with the same question I just asked you. The answer is also hiking, but I do love swimming. It's great exercise."

"That's not fair. You're supposed to answer the question you were given."

"Says who?" She smiles sweetly.

"The rules." I shrug like the answer is obvious.

A smirk graces her lips. "Archer. There are no rules."

"They are unspoken but very real rules when playing Twenty Questions," I say, leaning toward her.

She punches my shoulder. "You didn't answer my first question, so it's fair for me to skip one too."

Sparks riddle my body, and my shoulder burns where she touched. "Nope."

"Is that how you play on the field? Making up rules as you go?" She lightly shoves me backward as she stands.

"Maybe." I look up at her with a wicked grin. "Care to toss a ball around? You can see for yourself."

She holds her phone up. "Only if I can send a picture of you to my brother. He doesn't believe we've met."

"We can do better than that," I say before standing next to Clara. I smash our heads together as I swipe the phone from her hand. "Smile!" I snap a selfie before handing the phone back to her.

"He's gonna freak out." The smile she gives me is genuine.

So are the chills running down my arms.

—————— ❤ ——————

First thing the following morning, Clara and I meet the contractor, Vanessa Collins. Her crew will be here later this evening, so we decided to get a head start.

Clara shoves past me and picks up a hammer half her size. "I got dibs on knocking down the wall."

I follow her, half expecting I'd have to help, but she swings the hammer, taking a chunk out of the wall. "Wow."

"You must not be used to country girls," she says, sporting a smug expression.

"Guess not." In my mind, I've thought of her as more of a city girl. Until standing here watching her swing at the wall like it somehow offended her, and she's determined to retaliate.

A few hours later, we've moved on to stripping wallpaper from the kitchen cabinets. I glance at Clara as a drip of sweat lands in my eye. "Where do you get your energy?"

"Coffee and love."

I go really still. "Love?"

"Yes, you know love for life?" Her voice comes out

melodic.

The front door bangs open. Gagging sounds greet us as we venture into the living area. Jane holds her hand over her nose and mouth. "This place smells terrible. I don't get paid enough for this."

"I agree with Jane." Abigail backs out of the doorway. "We'll be back tomorrow morning."

Clara and I look at one another and burst out laughing, the tension of the moment dissipating into the air.

Chapter 23

Clara

With Archer back in Little Rock for a meeting, the internal conflict I have is going nowhere. My emotions are all over the place. One minute, I think he likes me, the next, I've convinced myself it could never work.

Loud music drifts through the open windows in my apartment. I listen for a minute before grabbing Mr. Bingley and joining them. Sweat pours down my neck after an hour of playing with the group.

I go upstairs, take a quick shower, and collapse on

my bed. It couldn't have been thirty minutes later when my phone rings. With a groan, I roll over and glance at my screen.

"Hey, Dad," I say. "What's up?"

"Don't panic, honey," he begins.

Can I say how much I panic whenever someone starts the conversation with don't panic? "What's happened?"

"Mom was in a car accident. She's on her way to St. Vincent's."

Oh no. I sit up straight before bouncing off the bed. "Is Gramma okay?"

"She's alive, but I don't know the details yet."

The wall comes out of nowhere and cracks me in the head as I bend over to pick up a pair of sweatpants. I need to slow down. "I'll be on my way in a few minutes."

"Please say a prayer. And be very careful driving." He sighs. "On second thought, why don't you wait and come in the morning?"

"No, I'm coming now. Let me call Jane."

"Okay. Love you, honey."

"Love you, too. Please keep me posted."

I call Jane and fill her in. She insists on driving me

because she thinks I sound panicked. For once, I don't argue.

It takes us right at four hours to get to Little Rock. When we pull in, Dad meets us in the parking lot. He hugs me and Jane and runs his hand over his balding head. "Mom's still in surgery."

"So, what happened?"

"We don't know all the details yet, but it was a one-car accident. Her car flipped, and she crawled out."

"Wow. What kind of surgery is she having?"

"Her liver is punctured and her pelvis fractured. They're working on the pelvis now."

A sob escapes me. I can't lose my gramma. She keeps me grounded. Jane loops her arm in mine as we continue to the waiting room.

As I step inside the bright hospital from the darkness, I blink a few times to adjust my vision. I blink again when I lock gazes with the last person I expect to see here: my mom.

She opens her arms wide, and I walk into her embrace for the first time in years. She gathers me close, and my tears flow. Perhaps this is the comfort I've been yearning for: the support from the one person I have refused to accept it from.

By morning, Gramma's low snores fill the ICU. I take Dad's hand after watching Jane and Mom leave to pick up Starbucks. "How did you move on from what Mom did?"

A hint of a smile brushes his lips. "I forgave her. Holding onto it would have just made me unhappy."

I look up at him. "What about now? Why is she here?"

He pins his arms over his chest as his smile slips away. "I knew she was in town for work, so I decided to give her a call."

I raise my eyebrows. "So, she's not staying with you?"

Dad chuckles, "Why do you ask that?"

"Just curious."

Gramma stirs. "Clara, your dad would be a fool to let your mama get away a second time."

"She's the fool for leaving him in the first place," I say as my lips slip into a frown. "I want to know why she's here. The real reason."

Dad opens his mouth but shuts it when someone pecks on the glass door. "Come in," I say.

Archer slides the door over a few inches and pokes his head inside.

My pulse quickens when I meet his blue eyes. "What are you doing here?"

"I hate to interrupt, but I wanted to check on everyone." His crisp silver-gray slacks and teal button-up fit him like a glove as he steps inside the room. "I found out about the accident after the board meeting."

Dad stands and extends his hand to Archer. "Anthony Sharp."

Archer takes Dad's hand. "Archer Banks, nice to meet you, sir. I'm sorry it's not under better circumstances."

"Same here," Dad responds, giving me a knowing look.

"How is she?" Archer asks as he steps close to the bed.

Gramma opens her eyes. "I'm doing much better now that you're here. Did you come to sweep my granddaughter off her feet?"

I moan. I don't know anyone else who could have liver and pelvis surgery and still have enough energy to play matchmaker.

I stand and guide a hesitant Archer out the door. "I'm sorry about that."

His lips quirk into a lopsided grin. "It's not a problem. I like how spunky she is." He takes my hands in his, and I may not be able to think straight. "Can I do anything for you? I have another meeting in thirty minutes, then I'll be free."

"No. We're good but thank you for stopping by." My hair is a rat's nest, and I haven't brushed my teeth since last night. I sure don't need Archer hanging around to see me at my worst.

"Call me if you need anything." He sticks his head back inside the room. "Don't worry, Gramma, I'll be back with my broom later."

Chapter 24

Clara

When I walk back into her room, Gramma has the nerve to wink at me. She's lucky I don't turn off her pain medication. Instead, I take her hand and sit beside the bed. "You know Archer and I are not interested in dating each other."

She scoffs. "I know for a fact that's a lie."

My face heats as I try to think of what to say. "It is not. Just because he's attractive doesn't mean anything." I turn to Dad. "Now you can finish telling me why Mom's here."

"Because I'm concerned about my mother-in-law's health," Mom says as she and Jane enter. Technically, the visitor limit is two, but Mom knows the charge nurse, so no one is saying anything about us being over.

"I asked her to come, Clara," Dad adds. Might I mention he sounds a bit too defensive for my liking? "She was already in Little Rock, so I thought she could give her opinion." And he seems to be trying too hard to explain.

I narrow my eyes as my gaze bounces from his to hers. Jane hands me a cup. "Here. Drink this and quit trying to overanalyze everything." I make a face at Jane as I take the cup of iced white chocolate mocha.

The door slides open, and Donny struts inside. He's three years younger than I am, but we look the same age. "What am I gonna do with you, Gramma?" he asks before kissing her cheek.

She tsks. "I misjudged how sleepy I was."

I nearly choke on my coffee. "Gramma! I thought it was an accident."

"It was."

Donny kisses Mom and wraps Dad in a bear hug before heading my way. "Clare Bear, I've missed you," he says as he hugs me. "Are you famous yet?"

"Hush." I nudge him on the shoulder. "I'll be famous as your sister when your band makes it big."

"True. By the way, I never got proof that you met Archer Banks," Donny says. "Is this another Johnny Cash situation?"

"I texted you a picture!" I say.

He scans his phone and cocks his head. "Huh. I missed it." He turns the screen around and shows everyone the selfie Archer took of us. "Is there something going on with you and Archer Banks? I expect to meet him, you know."

I ignore Donny. Jane barks a laugh. She was in on the Johnny Cash story.

Donny forgets about me and Archer as he gives Jane a once-over, letting out a low whistle. "Wow, I may have to move back to Mountain View if all the girls look as good as you."

Jane's brow creases, but she doesn't say anything. Her beet-red neck, however, speaks loud and clear. My brother has her flustered! I can't wait to give her a hard time over this when we're alone.

Gramma grins. "Oh, Clara is for sure sweet on him."

Donny cocks his head. "Hmm. I believe Gramma."

Mom clears her throat. "I still have the bedroom set up we used when Dad was fighting cancer." She tugs a bunch of hair behind her ear and looks at Gramma. "You're welcome to come to my house when they release you."

"I may take you up on that," Gramma says.

I grit my teeth. How are they acting like she didn't leave us for another man? That she didn't destroy my and Donny's childhood?

"I can't expect you to take care of Mom alone." Dad's tone is friendly, but there's something off about his body language – like maybe it's a little *too* friendly.

"Well, why don't you come stay with us?" Mom counters, a hopeful edge to her voice. "To help take care of Martha?"

Jane's right, I'm overanalyzing everything, even everyone's tones. My head starts to spin. What is even happening here? Why is no one else not acting like this is a big deal? I can't let this happen.

"Maybe we should *all* move back in." My overly sarcastic tone seems lost on everyone but Gramma, who gives me a dirty look.

Mom beams. "I think that's a wonderful idea."

"Clara may be onto something." Dad taps his chin.

Gramma gives me a smug look. The older she gets, the more smug she looks.

Donny cackles and wiggles his brows at me before throwing his arm around Jane. He lands a smile on her that most girls swoon over. "I'm game to move in if you are."

Jane doesn't swoon. She knocks his arm off and half smiles. "You're something else."

"I'll let my doctor know I'm transferring to Mountain View as soon as I can," Gramma says with a wince as she shifts in the bed.

Wait. That's not how this was supposed to go. As soon as Gramma is better, we're having a talk. I don't understand how she can want her son back together with the woman who abandoned him and their kids.

Mom and Dad start making plans about the move, seemingly forgetting that anyone else is in the room. Even though Jane and Donny won't be moving in, it looks like Dad, Gramma, and I will.

Good job, Clara. Maybe next time I'll think before speaking.

But probably not.

Chapter 25

Archer

I t's been over a week since I last saw Clara. We've texted back and forth, strictly so I can check on Gramma, of course.

My morning has been filled with meetings, and for some reason, Trevor asked to meet up with me. As I wait, my thoughts stay on Clara. What is it about her that keeps her on my mind? I've never had a woman control my emotions like her.

I tap on my screen.

My assistant, Summer, ushers Trevor inside my office.

He strides over to the wall of windows and sticks his hands in his pockets as he looks at the city. "I owe you an apology about the Clara situation."

"I appreciate that. If you lie to me again, I will not let it slide. Now, let's move on," I say, adjusting my posture in the chair, ready to shift our conversation to business.

"Yes, sir. I have to ask, is there something going on between you and Clara?" he asks as he walks over to my desk, claiming one of the leather chairs.

"What do you mean?" I ask, trying to maintain a calm demeanor despite the direction the conversation is going.

He crosses his legs, his expression becoming serious. "We're getting back together."

"Then why would you even ask that?"

"Just trying to gauge where you stand."

"Clara and I have been spending time together."

"That's going to have to change," he insists, his voice rising slightly.

"That'll be challenging, especially since I plan to see her more." I shoot back.

"She's my fiancée," he snaps.

"No, she's not." I suddenly feel foolish, sitting here arguing with Trevor like teenage, hormone-filled boys.

My impulse is to tell him to leave. Not only my

office, but the company. He's lucky he has my grand-father on his side.

His jaw tightens, but he quickly masks it. "Fine, how would you feel if I said I've been seeing Brianna?"

My gaze hardens. "First, I'd ask why you care about what Clara's doing if you're with Brianna."

"It's more a casual situation." With a sigh, he stands and shoves his hands in his pockets. "I have next week off, so I'll be in Mountain View winning Clara back, just so you know."

"I'll see you in Mountain View." I hear myself say. There's no way I'll let Trevor hurt Clara again. I narrow my eyes, contemplating a transfer to another state. For Trevor.

He walks to the door before turning back with a smirk. "May the best man win."

My gaze hardens as I pick up the phone, dialing Summer.

"Yes, sir?"

"Summer, do me a favor and set up a teams meeting with Mark Worthington for next week. I want to open up another director position on his team."

"Absolutely."

"Thank you," I say, with a smile. My mood is lifted

and I'm ready to tackle the pile of papers on my desk.

I wonder how Trevor will enjoy Alaska.

Chapter 26

Clara

Even though it's June, I breathe in the spring flowers in the early morning breeze. It's amazing how much I've missed Mountain View and how at home I feel here.

After a little over a week in the hospital, Gramma is on her way home. Since she's coming here, I'm back in Mountain View, ready to start designing.

I leave my apartment and load the last box into my car. If things were different, I'd for sure offer to buy the place, but now I'm doing something I never thought I would: packing to move in with Mom. I deserve a treat. The person working in the ice cream shop waves, and I take that as a sign to get a scoop of cotton candy ice cream.

A few minutes later, I sit on a bench and enjoy the sweet burst of cold yummy. Once done, I cross the street to where I'm parked and load my stuff inside.

After I shut the trunk, I turn around and gasp. Trevor is standing beside the passenger door. I blink a few times before finding my voice. "What are you doing here?"

He pulls his white polo shirt away from his chest, and his lips twitch into a smile. "Can we talk?"

"About what? I'm busy." I reply, glancing at my watch.

Just when my day couldn't get any more chaotic, Archer and his dad stroll up the sidewalk. Trevor's expression hardens, and he shoots me a glare. "Were you expecting company?"

Before I can respond, Archer beckons me over. "Hey, how's your grandma?"

"I was just about to ask about her," Trevor cuts in.

"She's on her way to Mom's," I reply with a sigh. "We all are."

"That's great."

While Paul engages Trevor in a conversation about golf, his favorite subject, Archer lowers his voice. "I have a proposition for you."

I'm intrigued but can't let him know exactly how much. "What's that?"

"Walk with me?"

Trevor is so engrossed in talking about golf that he doesn't notice Archer and I leave.

Archer scratches his neck. "Will you fake date me?"

I wrinkle my forehead as I have a hard time digesting what he just said. "Excuse me?"

"Wait," he says as he runs his hands through his hair. "That didn't come out right."

"Okayyy."

"Trevor has been seeing my ex, and I might've given him the impression you and I are spending time together."

I knew there was a reason Trevor was here. He doesn't want me but doesn't want anyone else to have me. "We *are* seeing one another. For work." Mostly for work. But also, for pleasure, I want to say, but don't.

Archer takes a step closer to me, which causes my

legs to go all wobbly. "Yeah, but he doesn't know what's going on between us," he says, jiggling his eyebrows.

"Look, I'm not lying about dating you. But I'll agree to tell everyone we've decided to get to know one another better." I close the space between us, planting myself a mere two inches from Archer.

I smile when he pulls a sharp breath in. Perhaps I affect him almost as much as he affects me.

A gulp causes the column of his throat to ripple. He runs a hand through his hair before landing a smile on me that could cause a nun to take a second look. "Can we start by telling Trevor now? He's only here because he thinks I'm interested in you."

I loop my arm in his. "There's nothing I'd like better." Archer's arm is warm against mine, and his muscles strain against my hand as we approach Paul and Trevor.

Their talk has simmered, and Paul steps away to take a phone call. Trevor's gaze goes straight to my arm looped in Archer's. "Clara, I hate how things ended with us. I'm here to make amends. I want you back."

I remember the pain Trevor caused me when he cheated, but I also remember the good times we shared. Seeing him now is difficult, especially with Archer by my side, knowing how easily replaceable I was to Trevor. It's embarrassing.

Not wanting to get into anything too heavy, I smile and say, "I really appreciate your effort to make things right, but getting back together isn't in the cards for us."

"Is it because of him?" Trevor's tone is low. He seems offended that I would dare to move on after he cheated on me.

"I can't believe you never mentioned you know Archer." I cross my arms over my chest. I'd rather be at Mom's than have this conversation.

"I didn't think it was relevant." He shrugs.

"You do know how much I admire him...as a football player, right?"

"Of course, I know!" He says, his face turning a light purple.

Now it all clicks. Trevor is jealous of Archer. How did I spend over a year with him and not see how self-focused he is?

"You still haven't answered my question. Are you and Archer dating?"

"All I can say is that we're getting to know each

other better.”

"Why? Because you're obsessed with him?" He looks at Archer as he opens the door to his sleek black Audi. "You better watch yourself, man. She might be your most obsessed fan. I'd hate to see anything bad happen to you."

Chapter 27

Clara

Despite the knots in my stomach, I pull into the circular drive at Mom's directly beside a medical delivery van.

Mom's modern two-story brick and rock home sits on the outskirts of Mountain View but would fit in with a Tuscany village. It's been a while since I've been here. Three years, to be exact.

I remember exactly what I was wearing when Mr. Avery told me I'd no longer be welcome here if my attitude didn't change. Oh, my attitude changed, alright. For the worse.

When I walked out that front door, I promised myself it would be a cold day when I returned. Yet here I am, ready to face the past for Gramma.

For Gramma, I keep reminding myself.

A man's laughter greets me when I enter the grand foyer through the dark wood and stained-glass double doors. Gramma is laid back in a plush recliner with a man young enough to be her son rubbing her feet.

What twisted reality have I walked into? "Um, Gramma? What're you doing?"

"Hey, Clara Dean," Gramma says. "Your sweet mama said a massage will be good for me." She wiggles her eyebrows and lays her head down. "And I'm inclined to agree."

That, at least, makes sense. "Where's everyone at?"

Gramma raises her head and glances out the back window. "I think your mama and dad are at the pool."

The pool? I drop my bag and march through the back door. Mom and Dad are lounging in chairs with their heads huddled together.

I clear my throat and stop at the end of Dad's chair. "What's up?"

Mom springs to her feet. "We're just talking." She

stammers. "Do you need some help bringing your things inside?"

"Nope. I have it all."

Dad excuses himself when his phone rings. I pin Mom with a stare, the tension between us palpable. "What are you up to?"

She brings her hand to her throat. "What do you mean, Clara?"

"You know what I mean, Mom. You better not be playing games with Dad."

"I wouldn't do that."

"Yeah, I also never thought you'd cheat on him. Until I saw it with my own eyes."

Dad comes back, interrupting our conversation. "Guess who that was."

I'm aggravated, so I'm not in the mood, but I somehow muster up a smile. "Who?"

"Ruby Sharp. Her and Tammy are in Mountain View and want to see us," he says with a smile, surprising me with the unexpected news.

I bounce on my toes as my mood quickly shifts. "That's great. Where are we meeting?"

"I told them they can come here," he says as he glances at his watch. "They'll be here in an hour or so."

"Oh, okay. Let me call Jane."

Sure enough, an hour later, an old school Ford Bronco pulls into the driveway. Dad lets out a low whistle before heading outside with Jane and me on his heels. "Nice ride."

"I call this Bronco Tammy's pride and joy." A blonde woman, who reminds me of a younger Dolly Parton laughs as she hugs Dad. "It's good to see you again." She stops in front of me and puts her arms out for a hug. "You favor my Tammy Gail."

Tammy Gail hops out with a solidly built Pitbull. Jane shrieks and steps behind Dad.

"He won't hurt you. His name is Castle, and he is a sweetheart," the woman I assume is Tammy comments.

Ruby is right. Tammy and I do favor a tad bit. And I'm not mad about it. This woman is a stunner who obviously can kick tail and take names.

After introductions, we head inside, where the massage therapist is packing up. Ruby and Mom enter the kitchen while the rest of us sit on the luxury sectional.

"So, Tammy, tell me what it was like to find a killer?" Jane asks, sounding a little awestruck.

"Considering I was racing against a clock to find my mama, it was heart-wrenching." Tammy scratches Castle's head, and he nudges her hand when she stops.

Jane leans forward, and her eyes widen. "Did you really stab him in the neck?"

Ruby chuckles as she follows Mom into the living room. "She sure did."

"Wow," Jane says.

"I hear congratulations are in order." Dad looks at Tammy. "Ruby says you're engaged to your high school sweetheart."

Tammy blushes and holds her hand out. "Thank you. I'm very happy."

Dad meets Mom's gaze. "There's nothing like re-connecting with the love of your life."

He sounds happier than he has in years. Watching him and her interact, I wonder if I'm wrong for not wanting them back together.

Who am I to try to stop love?

I think of my growing feelings for Archer and wonder if I should take my own advice.

Chapter 28

Archer

My heart seems to have a mind of its own when it comes to Clara Sharp. My brain tells me to back off. It says I have no time for romance. But my heart demands I run, no sprint, headfirst into a relationship.

But why? I wonder if it's because of the competition with Trevor with her being his ex but I quickly dismiss that idea. That fact would make me back off and not want to get to know her better. The jealousy I felt when I saw Clara and Trevor together yesterday left me reeling. This is not normal behavior for me.

I leave my room at the inn and descend the dark wooden stairs, anticipation for breakfast filling me. The owner makes the best cathead biscuits and gravy. I'd never even heard of those until coming here but I'll definitely be back for his breakfast.

Dad joins me at our table, which is set with vintage rose plates filled with eggs, bacon, biscuits and gravy and crystal glasses full of orange juice. He eyeballs me as he takes a bite of scrambled eggs. "What's going on between you and Clara?"

I choke on my biscuit. After coughing, I shrug. "I don't think she's ready for a relationship. Half the time, I'm not even sure if she likes me." My voice comes out scratchy.

Dad shakes his head. "She feels something for you. I can see it."

The orange juice I sip burns all the way down. "Yeah, I don't know"

"Trust me, son." He scoops up another bite of eggs. "Didn't y'all say you're getting to know each other better?"

"The only reason she agreed to that is to make Trevor back off."

"You should ask her to go to the awards banquet with you." Dad leans back in his chair with a grin.

"But that's in Little Rock. I doubt she'll want to return there after just getting back to Mountain View," I reply before staring out the window at an overcast sky.

"I bet you a dollar she says yes."

"Fine. I'll ask her," I concede, "but I'm pretty sure she'll decline."

"There's a spark there. I see it, and I have no doubt you feel it."

"More like a one-sided spark on my end," I say with a sigh as I cross my arms. My mind goes to the time I've spent with Clara, and I know I'm wrong. She feels something for me. I'm not exactly sure what yet, but I plan to figure it out.

Dad chuckles before taking another sip of coffee. "You're used to having women fawn over you. This is new to you, huh?"

"Do you think it's possible I like her because I can tell she's not as into me as most women?"

"No. You're not that petty," Dad reassures me.

"Ha, I sometimes wonder." I take a deep breath, preparing myself for the uncomfortable conversation

I'm about to have. "So, where do you see things going with you and Miss Bennett?"

"Abigail?" His face lights up as his mouth lifts into a soft smile. "Far. Why? Does that bother you?" he asks as his lips slip into a slight frown.

"Well, honestly, I can't see you two working out."

"What are you basing that assumption on?"

I take a deep breath, determined to choose my words with care. "Dad, you've had, what, four girlfriends since Mom passed away?" A heavy silence lingers as he lowers his gaze.

After what seemed like more than a minute, he meets my gaze. "I'm sorry if my dating life has hurt you, son. But I'm dealing with Maggie's death the best way I know how." He throws his napkin onto his plate and stands. "She made me promise to remarry. I didn't want to, but she said she couldn't bear dying and leaving me alone. I made that promise and will not lie to her." Tears pool on his lashes as he walks away.

I stand and follow him through the front door, stopping on the path filled with colorful flowers. "I just don't want to see you get hurt. Or hurt her. She's a nice woman."

"We both understand the stakes, and Abigail and I have decided that the potential for a chance at happiness far outweighs the risks. It's a gamble we're willing to take, even if it means we might end up alone."

He holds my gaze, his eyes compelling me to understand. "You need to open your heart and try to find love. What you decide now could change everything." With a firm squeeze on my shoulder, he steps away, leaving me to ponder the possibilities ahead.

As I watch Dad leave, I can't help but wonder if Clara Sharp is the one for me. And if so, how can we make things work?

Chapter 29

Clara

A mosquito buzzes in my ear, competing with Jane as she chatters about her phone call with Chance from last night.

I swat the mosquito as I half listen. Why can't I focus on what my best friend is saying?

Because Archer is standing on the wrap-around porch of his newly acquired cabin.

No, not just standing. He's tossing a football to a boy who looks like he is around ten or eleven. Every time he pulls the ball back to throw it to the kid, every muscle in his arm ripples against the white t-shirt he has on.

I have no earthly idea what Jane is saying.

As a matter of fact, I have no idea if I'm still breathing.

She stops next to me and follows my line of sight. "Oh my, I see why you're not listening to me."

"What?"

Before she answers, Archer's realtor, Sid, steps onto the porch, followed by Abigail. "Hey, son," he says to the boy playing ball with Archer. "Ready to go see your sister?"

The boy shrugs. "I'd rather stay here, Dad."

Sid ruffles his hair, and they say goodbye.

After they leave, Archer turns to me with a smile, his dimples on point. "Sid offered to show me another cabin down the road that's for sale."

Abigail, leaning against the doorframe with a playful smirk, chimes in. "And we would get to fix it up."

I raise an eyebrow, and my curiosity gets the best of me. "You plan on moving to Mountain View?" I ask.

Because if you are, I am.

No, I most certainly will not move for a man.

"This would make a good home," he says as he

glances around the yard, "or it could be an inn."

"An inn sounds great." I can't stop an image of Archer and me sitting around a fireplace in a cozy room, drinking cups of hot cocoa, from flitting through my mind.

What is wrong with me? I can't let my imagination get the best of me. Not when it comes to Archer Banks.

"Yeah, an inn for sure."

"I can picture that," I squeak out. Archer has no idea how vividly.

Jane bounds past us and disappears through the front door. "Come on, y'all," she yells from inside.

We spend the next hour going through the rooms, watching Abigail make sketches and take notes on her tablet. At least the skunk smell has died down.

Once Abigail is happy with the progress we've made on the design, she exits through the back with Jane close behind.

I half smile at Archer before walking toward him. He grips my arm. Heat from his hand shoots a thrill of I don't even know what to call it throughout my body.

"Dad thinks I should ask you to attend a banquet

with me in Little Rock that's coming up next week."

How does he expect me to form words when he's holding my arm like this? I stare at him for a good thirty seconds, trying to find my voice. Should I tell him how much I'd love to go to the banquet with him? That his blue eyes cause my heart to pound? Or how his touch leaves my skin tingling?

He lets go of my arm and raises both hands. "I told him you wouldn't be interested in traveling to Little Rock just to go to a banquet with me."

After our meeting at the restaurant, I would have said absolutely not. But now Archer has shown me a different side of himself. I look at him with a little smirk. "When is it?"

"Next Friday night, I figured we could stay overnight and then get up early to hike Pinnacle Mountain after breakfast Saturday morning."

My brows raise.

His face turns pink, and he shakes his head. "I'll stay at home, and of course I'll pay for you a hotel room."

Jane pokes her head inside the front door. "Hey Archer, will you give Clara a ride home? Mom and I have to do...something."

That little liar.

He grins. "Sure, it's no problem."

Jane slips out the door and hops into Abigail's Toyota Highlander before I can call her out on her lie. I bite my bottom lip and meet Archer's amused gaze. "You know she's lying, right?"

He shrugs. "It was pretty obvious."

A little later, we pull into Mom's driveway. Archer looks out the window, seemingly impressed. "What does your mom do for a living?"

I shrug. "She's a surgeon," I reply as I open the door. "Wanna come in and say hi to Gramma?"

"I'd love to."

As soon as we walk inside, a saucy, garlicky fragrance hits us, and my mouth immediately waters. If there's one thing I miss about my mom, it's her homemade lasagna. For once, I'm looking forward to dinner.

Mom walks around the sleek granite counter, wiping her hands on a towel. "Clara, I made your favorite." She stops in her tracks when she sees Archer.

Archer extends his hand. "You must be Clara's mother. I'm her good friend, Archer Banks."

My good friend? Why do those words make my mouth go dry?

Mom takes his hand. "Krystal. It's nice to meet you,

Archer."

Amazingly, she didn't make it weird.

Gramma buzzes into the room in a hover round. She looks at me. "Set another place for Archer at the table."

Archer opens his mouth, but Gramma stops him. "No arguing. You're staying."

"Yes, ma'am. It smells delicious, so there'll be no argument from me."

She grins, "Did you bring that broom we talked about?"

"I'm working on that."

"You hear that, Clara Dean? I expect you to cooperate." Gramma snickers.

If she only knew how badly I *want* to cooperate.

Chapter 30

Clara

The next morning, I wake up with cinnamon rolls on my mind. Maybe because the sweet aroma surrounds me. I bounce down the stairs just as Mom takes a pan out of the oven.

What is her deal? I open my mouth to ask, but when she turns around, there are tears in her eyes. I take a step closer. "What's wrong?"

She wipes her eyes and lets out a breath. "Please forgive me for wasting so many years we could've spent together, Clara. I'm begging you."

My heart lurches, and I nod as moisture spills through my lashes. I've waited a long time for this moment.

Yes, Mom has apologized before, but this time it feels different. I have her back, and I promise myself to never let anything come between us again. "I forgive you," I say as I pull her into a hug.

We stand here for a solid minute holding one another. "I promise I'll never leave you again, baby. Never. I wish I could go back and change things," she sobs.

"I know you won't," I say, tightening my arms around her. "We can move on from here, Mom. I want to."

She leans back, linking our eyes. "You have no idea what this means to me," she says, winding her arms back around me.

"Me, too."

Finally, she pulls back and smiles. "I can't believe you're dating Archer Banks."

"We're not technically dating."

"Bull. Y'all are dating. You just may not realize it."

I grin as I snag a cinnamon roll. "I gotta run. See you tonight."

"See you then, sweetheart. Have a good day."

On the way to Abigail's office, my mind is spinning overtime. Did my mom and I make up? With their divorce and now Mr. Avery in Colorado, I'm confident things will be better.

I turn the music up and smile when Gorgeous by Taylor Swift comes on. I can't keep a picture of Archer out of my head.

I sing along to the music at the top of my lungs until Jane calls. "Gooooood morning."

"Well, somebody is in a good mood."

"Yeah, I think my mom and I just made up."

Jane screams. "What? That makes me so happy." She repeats what I say to whoever is with her.

"I'm on my way to the office."

"Okay, I'll have you a coffee from Sasquatch."

Uh oh. One thing about Jane is she's a master briber when she wants something. "Who are you trying to set me up with now?"

"What? No one!" Her voice comes out high-pitched right before she laughs.

Yeah, she's up to something.

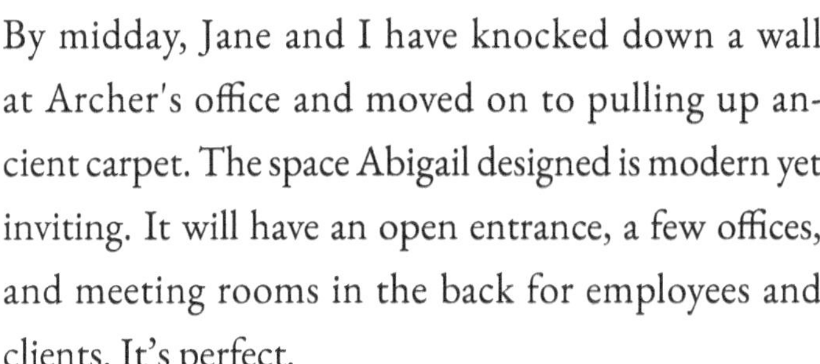

By midday, Jane and I have knocked down a wall at Archer's office and moved on to pulling up ancient carpet. The space Abigail designed is modern yet inviting. It will have an open entrance, a few offices, and meeting rooms in the back for employees and clients. It's perfect.

Archer walks in with Vanessa Collins, the contractor. He grins as he passes me, which causes my insides to flutter.

Vanessa inspects our handiwork. "Good job taking this wall down."

"Thanks, Vanessa," Jane says. "Did Mom tell you we plan to refinish the hardwood floors underneath the carpet?"

"Are you sure?" She rubs her chin and lands a sly grin on Jane. "I remember her saying to get rid of the hardwood and lay laminate."

"Har har. You've always thought you're a comedian," Jane teases, a playful smirk stretching across her lips.

"Listen, I need to run out to my truck. I'll be back in

a few minutes," Vanessa says, sticking her tongue out at Jane as she disappears out the front door.

"Hey, you," Archer says, his tone light and teasing.

"Yes," I blurt out.

"Yes, what?" he asks, raising an eyebrow, clearly amused by my response.

"I'll go," I say, my heart racing.

"To the banquet?" he asks, his eyes sparkling with intrigue.

"It's a date," I confirm, a mixture of excitement and nerves bubbling within me.

"A date, huh? That sounds good," he replies, grinning wider.

I glance at the door and gasp as I lock eyes with the same red-headed woman I caught kissing Trevor. She ignores me like I'm tar on the bottom of her tires after a road just got repaved.

Her lips curl into a smirk. "Hey, babe. I was told I could find you here."

Jane's head swivels so fast you'd think she was Beetlejuice. Her eyes widen as she meets my shocked gaze.

Archer narrows his eyes at Brianna before stepping close to me and entwining our hands. He shifts his eyes to her. "What can I do for you?"

Brianna speaks, and her voice is even more whiny than I imagined. "Can I speak to you alone for a minute?"

"You can speak in front of Clara and Jane."

Before Brianna responds, I lean into Archer and plant a kiss on his cheek. "We'll just run over to Sasquatch and grab some coffee. I'll bring you one back."

Archer kisses my temple like it's normal. Even though my heart starts pounding, my eyes snake up and down Brianna's tight outfit, and I snarl a smile at her as I pass by.

As soon as we're on the sidewalk, Jane gives me a high five. "I am so stinking proud of you right now."

I smile, feeling pretty stinking proud of myself.

Chapter 31

Archer

There could be no good reason for Brianna to be here. I gaze at her clingy dress with a sigh. Even though she is beautiful on the outside with her red hair and full lips, she is not the woman for me.

There was a time when I would have welcomed her visit. But those days ended when I overheard her telling her friend about how she was playing the field even when we were in a committed relationship.

"Why are you here?" I ask Brianna, but my gaze follows Clara.

"I need to speak to you about something important," Brianna says, her whiny voice grating my nerves.

"I can't imagine what." Clara just admitted we have a date, and that's all I want to talk or think about.

"Can we go somewhere? This is a sensitive matter."

"Just say what's on your mind." At the very least, I can hear her out since she drove so far. Not that I want to, but what else can I do?

"Two board members showed up at our house last night." She pauses, probably to make me ask why.

Brianna's mom is a member of the board of directors for Lombardi Enterprises, so I am curious, but not enough to probe. Her mouth pulls downwards into a pout before she continues. "Did you know your great-great-grandfather made a rule that no unmarried person can be the CEO?"

My stomach pitches as I try to digest what she just said. Surely, she's mistaken.

"Did you hear me?"

"I heard you." I tilt my head slightly, locking eyes with her. "But what brings you here?"

"Mom thinks I should do you a favor and marry you."

Of course she does. "I'm not marrying you, Brianna," I say as I take her elbow and lead her onto the sidewalk. It's time for her to go.

She stomps her foot and juts her bottom lip out. "Just think about it. We were good together, Archer. I'd hate for you to lose the company you love because you're too prideful to admit you made a mistake when you broke up with me."

She takes a few steps toward her black Range Rover before turning around. "Call me when you've come to your senses."

My mind whirls as Dad and I drive to Little Rock. After excusing myself, I left Clara and Jane looking bewildered. I hated to leave like that, but I have to find out if Brianna's mistaken. Is it possible to force someone to get married?

I'll engage my attorneys, but I must speak to Grandfather first. Dad glances at me. "Every CEO before you has been married, so this has never come up."

I pass a Dodge Durango going fifteen below the speed limit. "We need to read the document and have our attorneys review it."

"That's the plan, son."

We pull into Grandfather's driveway as the sun sets in the sky. I take a moment to admire the pink and yellow beauty and gather my thoughts before going inside.

Betsy greets us with a smile. "Good evening. I will be right back with some refreshments."

"Rebecca Leigh has already called me. She says you rejected her daughter's proposal." Grandfather looks at me with sharp eyes.

"You knew?" I ask as I rub my sweaty palms on my jeans.

"Only recently." He raises a wrinkled hand when I start to say something. "Brianna may be your only choice."

"I am not marrying that woman, Nonno."

"Do you have someone else in mind?"

A picture of Clara bounces around my mind, but I shut that thought down. There's no way in the world she would marry me right now.

Dad clears his throat. "You should ask Clara Sharp."

Betsy gasps as she sets down a picture of tea. "Sharp? Is she kin to Detective Tammy Sharp?"

"She's her cousin or something," I say.

"Then I agree. You must marry this woman," Betsy says this with the confidence of Simon Cowell judging hopeful singers.

Is my love life really up for discussion? "You're just fangirling over the detective." I grin.

"Yes, I'll admit this." She glances at her watch. "But for now, I need to pick up my son. You gentlemen have a good evening."

"You, too, Betsy."

She pauses at the door. "If you marry Detective Sharp's cousin, I expect you to save me a seat at the wedding."

Chapter 32

Clara

I've never considered myself a super nosy person, but I am absolutely dying to know what Archer is doing in Little Rock.

He's been gone for two days now, and it's driving me crazy.

And who is this Brianna woman? Is it possible she knows me and has some sort of vendetta to steal every man I'm attracted to? First, Trevor and now Archer.

Abigail found out from Paul that they're definitely not dating.

So, there's that at least.

A little voice in my head insists Archer and I are also not dating. And I understand that. At least my brain understands, my heart, not so much.

I wave at a man driving by in a tractor as I pull away from Archer's cabin. The contractors have been working around the clock to prepare it for opening. Archer plans to turn it into a rustic, small inn, which is a good idea.

A few miles down the road, a loud pop comes from the back of my car, interrupting my pondering.

What could that be?

Within seconds, the back tire flops, and I groan. I do not have time for a flat tire.

Thankfully, there's a decent amount of space to pull onto the side of the road.

I swap my heels for flip-flops in the back seat and make a mental note to add sweatpants and a t-shirt for next time.

Slacks and a silky blouse are not the best outfit to change flats, but I'll work with what I've got.

I grab my phone and share my location with Jane since she's at the office with Abigail and they're expecting me.

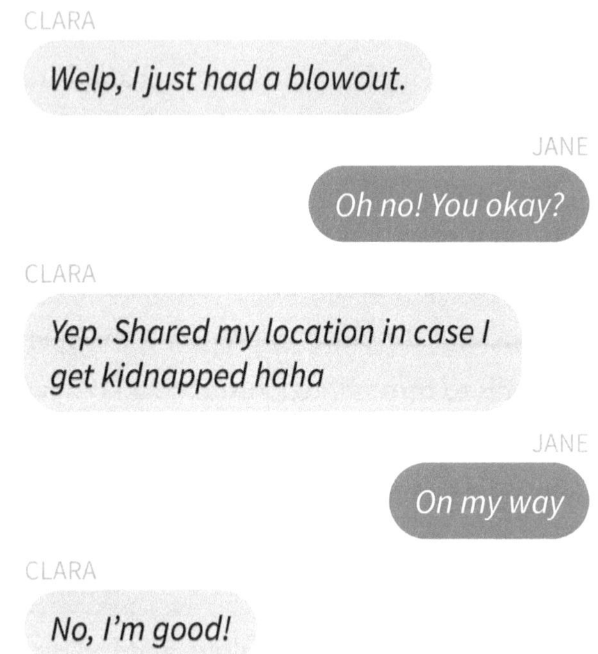

I stash my phone in my back pocket, grab the jack, lug wrench, and spare tire from the trunk, and get to work removing the lug nuts.

I don't think I'll get kidnapped, but I stay alert and keep my pepper spray handy. Within a few minutes, a vehicle pulls over behind mine, and I stand.

A tingle spreads throughout my body as I lock eyes with the man who has been occupying my thoughts all day.

His grin only grows wider the closer he gets to me. I can't help but notice how his loose white polo button-up flows onto his light blue and white checked shorts. I'm hyper aware of his every move, and I may or may not kiss him.

Okay. I may not. I will not. Instead, I return his smile before wiping the beads of sweat off my lip. "I hit something."

"That's what Jane said."

That little stinker. "She called you?"

"No, Dad and I just got to the office when you messaged her."

He holds his hand out and smiles wider, if that's possible. "Let me help."

My right hand goes to my hip. "I know how to change a flat."

"Obviously, but what kind of gentleman am I if I stand here while you do all the work?"

"Fine," I say as I hand him the lug wrench.

He sets it by the tire and starts unbuttoning his shirt. My cheeks grow hot, and I spin around. He laughs. "I have a t-shirt under this, Clara. No need to get all embarrassed."

"I'm not embarrassed."

Archer changes the flat faster than I ever could. Once he gets the spare on, he puts the flat tire and tools in my trunk. "I'll follow you to the tire shop."

"You don't have to do that."

"No arguments, please."

"You're impossible." I prop my back on the car.

He leans toward me. I hold my breath as his face gets close. What is he doing? I imagine him leaning down on one knee and professing his undying love before pulling me into an embrace. Every skin cell tingles when his gaze drops to my mouth. A sigh escapes as I wait.

Instead of proposing, he reaches a hand out, brushing a long curl away from my face before grabbing his shirt. The side of his mouth quirks upward as he shrugs his shirt on and buttons it. Meanwhile, my heart feels like it just catapulted down the side of the mountain we're on.

What is happening? I never felt this with Trevor, even though we were engaged. How does Archer have the power to make my senses go haywire?

Maybe it's time to stop fighting how I feel. But what if it's too late? What if he decided to get back together with Brianna? "Are you off the market?"

"Huh?"

"Did you and the girl who came here the other day

get together? Or back together?"

"Brianna? Absolutely not." He leans against my trunk directly beside me, his narrowed eyes somehow still staring a hole through me. "Why do you ask?"

I really wish I had the nerve to tell him how I feel, but I don't want him to think I'm some crazy stalker fan, like Trevor said. I shrug. "Call me nosy."

"I'd rather call you interested," he says, his eyes crinkling into a smile.

Why are my pits sweating like it's a hundred degrees out? Sure, it's around eighty, but it feels nice. "Okay, I'm interested." I hear myself say, then I add, "in getting a cup of coffee from Sasquatch. Want to join me?"

A laugh bursts from him. "A cup of coffee sounds great as long as it's cold."

Even though I'm sweating, shivers cover my arms.

It's official. I'm obsessed.

Chapter 33

Archer

The tire shop is closed, but the owner said he could get the tire fixed in an hour. This is why I love small towns. I glance at Clara, who's perched in my passenger seat, looking at her phone.

"What do you say we grab coffee and some sandwiches, then have a picnic?"

She taps her chin and puckers her lips out. "Hmm. Dad took Gramma to the doctor today, and Mom is home with a migraine. You up for hanging out at the pool?"

"That sounds good," I say. Not sure how I manage to play it cool with my pulse racing like it is.

Thirty minutes later, we lay out a small feast on the patio table. I take inventory of the space. The back-yard is phenomenal, featuring a slide, soaking area, and a rock waterfall that flows into the crystal-clear pool, all surrounded by lights.

After we eat and clean up, Clara glances at me. "Do you want to swim?" she asks.

"I don't have a suit."

"We have extra swim shorts and shirts."

"Okay."

She disappears into what I suspect is the pool house and comes out with shorts and a shirt. "Here you go. You can change in there."

The suit fits me perfectly. I normally don't wear a shirt in the pool, but I feel like she wants me to. Why else would she have brought it out? I lean by the edge of the pool and dip my hand in the water. It feels good.

I swivel my head when the back door shuts. Clara comes out of the house, and my breath catches in my throat. Why? I'm not sure.

It's not like she's wearing a skimpy bathing suit. Her pink swim shorts stop at her knees, and she's in a long-sleeved matching top. I've heard about women who dress modestly, and I never thought I'd be interested.

But boy was I wrong.

I'm staring. She probably thinks I'm a weirdo. My nerves kick in and I blurt the first ridiculous thing I can think of. "You trying to hide something?"

I'm not sure why I asked that question.

"No. How my body looks is my business."

"Oh, I know. I didn't mean to imply otherwise."

She marches up to me, and I open my mouth to apologize for ogling her and for the stupid question.

Before I get a word out, she shoves me, and I go flying into the pool.

On the way down, I grab her leg, and she tips over right behind me. We come up spitting out water and laughing.

She holds onto my shoulders with one hand and wipes her hair from her face with the other.

I breathe out an easy laugh. In this moment, it doesn't matter if I stay CEO or return to football.

All that matters is making the woman beside me smile. I stare into her eyes and wonder if I should say what's on my mind right now. I decide I don't have much to lose, so I say it. Or a version of it.

"I want to spend more time with you."

"Glutton for punishment?" she asks as she swims to the other side of the pool. "Or is it the shorts?"

"I guess a little of both," I reply with a grin.

We spend the next hour sliding and racing and getting to know each other better. Even though my free time used to be filled with A-lister parties and dinners, this is the most fun I've had in a long time.

After our third race from one end of the pool to the other, we collapse onto floats.

My float seems determined to stay near Clara's. I turn my head and notice she's staring at me. "Hi."

"Hi." She sounds out of breath, and that's a problem for my heart rate.

She stares at the waves between our floats and dips her fingers into the water. I dip my hand next to hers to see if she jerks away.

She doesn't. I'm feeling brave, so I wrap her pinky finger in mine. We float around for another few minutes just holding pinkies.

And I'm here for it.

Chapter 34

Clara

Jane and I spend the next few days focusing on the cabin design while Abigail works on the downtown office space.

We are all excited about the upcoming banquet, a rare occasion for us to dress up and socialize outside of our usual work settings.

My phone buzzes as I pull up at home the night before the banquet. Jitters line my stomach when I see Archer's name on the screen.

I've tried to avoid him since we held hands, or I

guess pinkies, the other night.

How can I allow myself to fall for him anymore than I already have? My heart is on the line, and I don't know what to do.

So, I figured I could take a few days to think things over.

The weight of my emotions is overwhelming, and I'm torn between my feelings and the fear of getting hurt.

Unfortunately, I'm still obsessed.

I drop my head onto my steering wheel and groan before reading the message.

ARCHER

Are you avoiding me?

CLARA

Why would you ask that?

ARCHER

Every time I come around, you leave.

CLARA

Ha, just been busy.

Busy, trying to control my emotions, but he doesn't have to know that. He probably thinks I'm super focused on getting his inn ready.

The following morning, I pile into Abigail's Highlander with Jane, and after stopping for coffee, we start for my apartment in Cabot.

The sun is just beginning to rise, casting a warm glow over the landscape. "I'm so glad we are all going to the banquet," I say, taking in the scenery.

"Me, too." Abigail smiles, her eyes sparkling with excitement.

I grip the back of the seat and glance at Jane, who turns to me, looking like she has a lot on her mind. "You never told me why you tried to bribe me with coffee the other day."

After taking a large drink of her iced mocha, Jane lifts her chin toward me. A gentle puff of a laugh floats from her. "I thought you needed bribing to go to the banquet, but it turns out you didn't."

A picture of Archer in a tux swims around my vision and I offer up a grin. "True, but I'm always down for coffee from Sasquatch."

Both Jane and Abigail bob their heads.

"Are you excited to see Chance?" I ask before draining my own iced mocha.

Jane gives a half-shrug, her gaze drifting out the window like she's searching for something on the side of the road. "Yeah, I guess." I get the impression she's struggling with her feelings for Chance.

"Is there trouble in paradise?" Abigail probes as she cocks her head while keeping her eyes on the road.

Jane sighs. "He's interviewing for a job in Arizona of all places," she says as she looks away from the landscape.

"Arizona?" I echo, surprised he's willing to move so far away. I thought he had stronger feelings for Jane.

"Yeah," Jane continues, her fingers fidgeting with the hem of her t-shirt. "There's a director position out there, and he thinks it'll be a great opportunity to advance in the company."

"Hmm. Sounds to me like you're not that into him." I hear myself say what I was thinking out loud.

"He's cute and sweet," Jane admits as she gives me the side eye, "but I don't feel a zing whenever I see him."

"A zing?" Abigail looks puzzled.

"Yes, you know, like Mavis had for Johnny in Hotel Transylvania," Jane explains, her brown eyes brightening momentarily.

"Don't try to force it then."

"I do like him, y'all don't get me wrong."

"Maybe you're concerned about getting hurt if he moves to Arizona," Abigail suggests, her brow furrowing.

"We'll see. I'm keeping my options open for now."

"When you find love, don't let it slip away."

Our conversation moves to how we're almost finished with Archer's projects, but my mind dwells on Abigail's words: when you find love, don't let it slip away.

I can't help but wonder if that is exactly what I'm doing.

Chapter 35

Archer

It's been four days since Clara and I had the moment in the pool. Four long days of me dreaming about touching her. It doesn't matter if it's day or night, she fills my thoughts.

That's why I could kick myself for agreeing it made sense for her to ride here with Dad, Abigail, and Jane. My skin tingles just thinking about what she's wearing. The internal struggle is real, and I'm torn between my desire for Clara and the fear of losing her.

Chance struts into the convention center foyer,

looking sharp in a light brown suit. "Hey, cuz. Thanks for inviting me."

"Not a problem, man. I figured you'd want to see Jane."

He runs a hand through his blonde hair and sighs. "I do want to see her, but I don't think she's as into me as I am her."

"What makes you think that?" I say after greeting Susan, one of our HR Managers, as she passes by with her husband.

He waits until Susan is out of earshot before he continues, "You remember me telling you about the job transfer?"

"To Arizona?"

"Yeah. She's not acting like she wants a long-distance relationship." He shrugs like he's indifferent. Maybe he is.

"Have you considered staying here?"

"No, this transfer will open up more opportunities in the company."

"Is that more important than Jane?"

He winces. "Hey, not all of us are born CEOs. I have to do whatever it takes to make it to the top."

"You didn't answer my question."

He shifts from one foot to the other. Before he answers, Clara walks into the foyer.

Our eyes meet, and a sense of weightlessness overtakes me. The black gown fits against her creamy skin with huge, layered ruffles flowing from her waist to her ankles. Her gown appears silky until she gets close, and I notice the detailed flower stitching and matching heels. I swallow the lump in my throat and try to breathe.

My gaze falls to the gold clutch, elegant bracelet on her tiny wrist, and I lose the breath I'd worked so hard to get. She stops in front of me and curtsies before grinning. Her eyes are a brilliant green, and I have no doubt I'd exchange a million dollars for her smile. This dress was made for her.

"You look stunning," I say, my tone soft and gentle.

With a blink of her eyelids, she examines me from head to toe. I can't help but squirm as I think about my simple black tuxedo. Hopefully, she likes what she sees.

The moment she tangles her gaze with mine, her eyes tell me she likes it. "You look nice."

I jump when Grandfather clears his throat. He must've snuck up on me. "Hello, Clara. Do you remember me?"

Recognition crosses her face. "I feel like we met at a restaurant somewhere. Where do I know you from?"

"We did indeed meet one time when you and Trevor were first dating."

"That's right. You're friends with his grandfather."

"Yes." He rubs his chin and glances from me to Clara. "I'm glad you're here with my grandson. You make a fine-looking couple."

Clara opens her mouth to respond, but clamps it shut as Grandfather walks away, chuckling. I shrug and offer her my arm. "Shall we?"

She glances at Abigail and Jane, who are standing, talking with Chance and my Dad, and nods. "We shall."

Clara leans next to my ear and whispers, "The decorations are lovely."

I shiver and glance around, trying to see through her eyes. Each table features white layered tablecloths, a massive floral arrangement, and white and gold place settings that complement the overall look. It is nice. "I agree," I whisper back.

We spend the next hour eating and watching companies win awards for outstanding community service. Ours was for having the highest number of employees who volunteered.

When Clara and Jane excuse themselves for a bathroom break, Grandfather elbows me. "Betsy's right, that's the girl you need to marry."

I grunt, but as I watch Clara retreat, every fiber of my being knows I'd love to be married to Clara Sharp.

Chapter 36

Clara

This night couldn't be more perfect. Well, I could do without seeing Trevor, but at least he's at another table. He keeps eyeballing me, but I am happily ignoring him.

I run my hands over my dress still unable to believe Mom had this dress waiting for me at my apartment. I had brought a really pretty green dress I once wore to a work event, but this one is gorgeous. Moisture covers my lashes as I think about how far we've come in the past couple of weeks. I feel like we are well on our way to having the relationship that moms and daughters should have.

I take the last bite of my roasted chicken breast, savoring the smoky sauce. If I were alone, I'd be scraping the mashed potatoes off the plate or even licking them. I giggle just thinking about it.

Archer raises a brow and leans close. "What's so funny?"

"I was just thinking about licking my plate clean," I whisper in his ear, which I've been doing a lot tonight.

He throws his head back into a full-blown laugh. "I'll give you a hundred dollars to do it."

I tap my chin as I consider the offer. There is a pair of ballet flats at Dillard's I've had my eye on. "No way."

"Two hundred?" he whispers in my ear, sending a volcano of heat down my neck to my fingertips.

Jane lands a knowing smile on me, and I smile back. Her grin turns mischievous right before she asks, "What are you two whispering about?"

All eyes shift to me and Archer.

"Mashed potatoes," Archer answers with a straight face.

I giggle again until Archer wraps my hand in his under the table. A pleasant hum warms my blood as I entwine our fingers. In Pride and Prejudice, Charlotte told Lizzie a man needs encouragement when fictional Jane Bennett and Mr. Bingley were talking. I feel the need to take her advice. From this moment on, I will encourage Archer.

He angles a glance at me, and I meet his gaze. Archer Banks is not what I expected. He's way more. He's someone I want to spend time with. A lot of it. Every day. Can this work out? Because my heart is saying it has to.

After the awards ceremony, everyone who came to support Lombardi Enterprises gathers on the sidewalk in front of the convention center. Even Trevor. Archer clears his throat. "Thank you to everyone who came out tonight. I appreciate your hard work and dedication to not only our company, but our community," he says as he hands the employees an envelope.

One of the women who works in the downtown office lets out a happy squeal. "Yes! A gift certificate for a massage!"

Trevor heads our way, stopping in front of me. "I'd like to give you a ride home."

I snort a laugh. If he'd tried this hard when we were engaged, we'd probably be married by now.

Next to me, Archer's back tenses right before he drapes a possessive arm around my shoulder. "We'd take you up on your offer, but what would I do with my car?"

Trevor takes a step toward Archer, his body tense. He jabs his finger in Archer's chest. "I'll tell you what you can do with your stupid car."

Archer grabs Trevor's hand, twisting it quickly and forcefully. "What would that be, Trevor?"

"Let go of me, man!" Trevor cries out.

Archer releases Trevor's hand and shoves him a few steps away. "You need to back off."

"I think we should let Clara decide who she's riding home with," Trevor continues, apparently feeling brave.

As I observe Archer and Trevor, a thought tugs at my mind: does Archer see me as something more than just a trophy in this game against Trevor? Out of nowhere, my stomach churns, and the voice of my internal insecurities takes over. There's no way Archer Banks is really interested in me.

"Thank you both for the offer, but I'm riding with Jane."

My dress swishes as I walk away, pride totally intact.

I barrel into my apartment as fast as my dress will allow. Jane follows me into the bedroom and puts her hand on her hip. "Why didn't you ride home with Archer?"

"Because," I say as I turn my back to her. "Unzip me, please."

"I'll never understand how you think," she replies as she unzips my dress. "I think you're in your head again. That's why you didn't ride with him."

"I am not," I say, shrugging out of the dress. "I think I'm another way for Archer to get at Trevor."

"See! I knew you were in your head." She shakes her head as I slip on my fuzzy pajamas.

"I don't want to get hurt again. Now turn around so I can unzip you."

"I think Archer likes you a lot."

"We'll see. I love your dress, by the way."

Jane stayed true to her eighties fashion by wearing a pink gown with puffy sleeves. "Thank you, my dear."

Abigail pounds on the door, causing us both to jump. "You two want to watch House Hunters with me?"

A few minutes later, we pile onto the reclining sofa with a smiling Abigail. I guess it beats crying myself to sleep over my stupidity.

Chapter 37

Clara

The following morning, we make it back to Mountain View early after Abigail wakes us up with the chickens. My stomach growls so I slip inside the house and go straight to the kitchen.

"Good morning, dear," Dad says, looking up from the newspaper he's reading at the dining room table.

Mom sets a plate of eggs, bacon, gravy, and biscuits on the table. She glances at me. "You hungry, Clara? We're having a late breakfast."

"I am." I twiddle with the belt loop on my Levi's.

"Thank you again for the lovely gown." I take a tentative step forward and then another until I'm in front of her.

"You're welcome."

I wrap my arms around her and feel her back stiffen before she relaxes and gathers me close. We stand like that for a few minutes, soaking in our recent relationship change. It's so fresh for us both.

I step back and pull a curl behind my ear. Dad and his plate of food are gone.

"I love you, Clara. It means so much…" her voice breaks.

"I love you, too."

My phone rings from inside my purse. I dig it out and frown as I greet my former boss. "Hey, Charles. What's up?"

"Clara! I have a job for you."

Well, that's not what I expected. "What kind of job?"

"There's an Operations Analyst position opening in Mobile, and you're a shoo-in."

"Oh really?"

"I'm not going to put you on the spot, so I'll give you a day to consider it. Call me tomorrow evening, and I'll get you an interview."

"So, I'm not a shoo-in?"

"Oh, trust me, you are, but they still have to interview you. You know how it is."

"Got it. I'll definitely think it over and let you know tomorrow," I reply, feeling a mix of curiosity and anxiety.

Both Mom and Dad are standing beside me, their expressions concerned as I wrap up the call. I share the details with them before heading to Abigail's office.

An hour later, I take a breath, bracing myself before I give the news to Jane and Abigail. After my speech, I lower my eyes when Jane frowns. "No way. You living in Cabot is tough enough. I can't handle the thought of you in another state."

"I agree with Jane," Abigail chimes in, her tone sad but supportive. "But I will stand by whatever choice you make."

"Thanks, Abigail." I nudge Jane playfully with my elbow. "Alabama is on the way to the beach, so we'll have lots of girls' trips."

"No, we won't because you'll be working all the time again," Jane retorted, a knowing pout on her lips.

She has a point, and I can't help but feel a twinge of

guilt. Not only for leaving my best friend, but I feel like this is the first time my mom and I have made any sort of progress. "I honestly don't know what I'm going to do yet."

"I know you'll keep us posted," Abigail said as she brushes off her jeans. "Are y'all ready to put the final touches on the design at the cabin?"

We're just about finished with both projects. This week, we'll finalize the last few details at the cabin before turning our attention completely to helping Abigail finish the office.

Then Archer will be free to disappear from my life. Unless he chooses to stay.

Chapter 38

Clara

After a long day of setting up the furniture in four guest rooms and the cabin's entertainment room, I only want to sleep.

I sneak into the house. Gramma snores from the recliner, which makes me giggle. She opens one eye before wagging her finger at me and nodding back off.

Mom walks into the living room still wearing scrubs. "Did you see your roses?"

"Huh? What roses?" I ask as shivers of excitement travel down my body. If Archer sent me roses, I may die here and now.

Mom's next statement deflates my daydream. "They're from Trevor."

Gramma raises her head. "I never liked that boy. Throw them in the trash and don't look back, Clara Dean."

I'm inclined to agree. At least after catching him cheating on me.

I read the card before pitching it in the trash. "I long to reconnect soon, Love Trevor."

Yeah, we'll be reconnecting, maybe never.

I dial his number on the way to my bedroom. He answered on the first ring. "I knew you'd be calling."

"Trevor."

"Do you like the roses?"

"They're pretty," I admit as I slip my shoes off, "but you shouldn't have sent them."

"Why not?"

I sigh. Why do I have to explain this? "We broke up, Trevor."

"That was a mistake."

I clench my jaw. "You cheated on me," I say, my voice sharp as the memory of seeing him kiss another woman assaults me.

"A misunderstanding," he insists, as if trying to dismiss what happened.

"Listen," I say, trying to maintain my composure, "I only called to ask you to stop. We are not getting back together."

There, I said it. Now he will have no choice but to leave me alone.

"Why not? Do you really think you have a chance with Archer? He's so messed up; he's trying to transfer me to Alaska."

"It doesn't matter either way. We will not be getting back together, regardless."

"Well, I hope you know he's getting fired as CEO."

"I don't believe you."

"Archer is getting replaced since he's unmarried. It's some sort of clause his great-grandfather set forth before he died. Only married men can be CEO."

"That's ridiculous."

"So, he'll either marry Brianna or leave the company."

My stomach knots as a vision of Archer wearing a tux, waiting for Brianna to walk down the aisle, assaults me. "Marry Brianna?"

"I can't blame him. I would marry her before giving

up a CEO position."

"Look, I need to go."

"You don't think he'll marry you, do you? Because it would only be to stay CEO. I hope you realize that."

Without another word, I end the call and put my phone on the bed. Feeling gross, I jump in the shower and scrub my skin raw.

After several minutes, I wrap my hair in a towel, throw on a sweatsuit, and head downstairs. I stop in my tracks when I come face to face with Archer sitting on the sofa, talking with Gramma.

He swivels around, and I catch my breath. He has the beginnings of a beard, and his messy, yet perfect hair looks like it hasn't been cut in a couple of weeks. I have a flashback of Archer in his football uniform, and my feelings overwhelm me. Still, I play it cool. "Hey."

His jogger shorts show tanned legs. I quickly look away when he catches me staring.

"Hey. Sorry for stopping by without an invite, but I was in the neighborhood and thought I'd see if you wanted to go to the movies." He grins at Gramma, and that zing Jane was talking about the other day slams through my body.

"Sure," I say without even thinking twice. He's going to think I have no life. "I mean, I guess. When are you thinking?"

"Now would be good."

The idea of watching a movie with Archer makes me forget I was just worrying about him believing I have no life. I think he knows that by now anyway. "Let me get ready. But we're taking my car."

He laughs as he looks me up and down. "Fine. And you look great, just maybe take the towel off your head."

I stick my tongue out at him before taking the stairs two at a time.

Chapter 39

Archer

Gramma pats me on the knee. "I'm happy to see you finally showing initiative and going after the girl."

I lean close to her, glancing between her and the stairs. "Is that right?" I ask, smiling to myself.

"That's right. My Don knew he wanted me and did what it took to make it happen. You should be more like him."

"Are you going to tell the story? You can't leave me hanging."

She grins and looks out the window, seemingly transported to another time. "I worked for the telephone company. Don managed a farm, and he needed to get through to the feed store. We had to wait for an open line, so we talked for a few minutes."

"Did you already know one another?"

"We didn't. But before we hung up, he asked for my last name, and I told him I couldn't share that information," she says with a big smile.

"He knew the supervisor, so he called and talked my boss into telling him who I was."

"Really?"

"Yes, and he followed me home that night after my shift ended," she shakes her head as a chuckle escapes.

I imagine Clara calling the police on me the night we met if I had followed her home. "Really?"

"Yes, he was bold. He pulled in behind me, and I asked him what he was doing."

"What did he say?" I ask, completely invested in the story.

"He introduced himself as Don and explained how my boss had shared my contact information with him. After a brief exchange of pleasantries, he boldly asked if I'd like to join him for a milkshake at a nearby diner."

"Did you go?"

"I told him it would be best if he came inside to ask my dad for permission first."

"Oh, did he actually come inside?"

"He certainly did! Don stepped into our living room, and the moment he spotted my dad's trophy deer mounted on the wall, his eyes lit up. They immediately struck up a conversation about hunting techniques and their favorite spots in the woods."

She pauses, chuckling at the memory. "Dad allowed me to go out for that milkshake."

"I can't believe he had the courage to follow you home."

"At the time, I couldn't either. Little did I know that phone call would blossom into a lifelong partnership. We got married, welcomed a wonderful son into our lives, and God blessed us with nearly fifty beautiful years together."

She scratches behind her ear, readjusting in her seat. "Don was determined from the start; he knew he wanted me and took the initiative to make it happen. So, I have to ask, you gonna muster that same courage?"

A pang strikes my insides as I meet Gramma's intense gaze. Before I can speak, Clara clears her throat. "Ready?"

I steal a glance at Clara, my pulse pounding in my ears. She's changed into a pair of black joggers and an oversized t-shirt. Her hair is styled in a bun on top of her head.

"Thank you for sharing your story. It means a lot to me," I say to Gramma as I bend down for a hug.

Her lip ticks up at the edge. "You two have a good time."

When Clara maneuvers her car into a spot in the second row at Stone Drive-In, my stomach rumbles, and I grin. "You hungry?"

"I will never turn down a burger from here." She looks into my eyes earnestly. "Never."

I open the door before glancing back at her. "Then what are we waiting for?"

Vibrant orange, pink, and blue hues fill the sky above the tree line and the large movie screen as we settle into our lawn chairs with our burgers, chips, nachos, and lemonade.

My mouth waters as I tune the portable radio to 90.3. I close my eyes and bite into my burger, savoring the small-town dairy bar taste that takes me back to my youth. It has the perfect amount of juiciness mixed with spicy cheese and mustard.

We eat in a comfortable silence as the live-action Lilo and Stitch plays on the giant screen.

I try to focus on the movie, but my mind keeps returning to what Gramma said. Do I have enough courage to pursue a real relationship with Clara? There's no doubt I do want to spend time with her. My mind stays on her when we're not together.

Women have always come easily to me. I've never had anyone push back like Clara does. Or drive me crazy. Or make my pulse hammer out of control.

She crunches a nacho chip piled with cheese and a jalapeno and glances at me. "What are you thinking about so intently?"

"Nothing, why?" I ask way too quickly. There's no doubt I sound guilty of something.

"Okay then." Her eyes sparkle like she knows exactly what I'm thinking. "Do you have to get married to keep your company?" she asks, which takes me by surprise.

"That's a long story. Think we can talk about it some other time?"

She nods, but I can tell she's curious. I'll need to fill her in soon.

After the trash is tucked away in a bag, I entwine our fingers. My breathing picks up when Clara rubs her thumb across the back of my hand to my wrist.

She scoots close to me. So close our mouths are within the same breathing space.

I hold my breath and angle my head to stare into her eyes. We both lean in, and I press my lips onto the side of her mouth. She changes her angle until our lips meet.

We stay completely still with our lips pressed together for a minute. It's almost like we're both afraid to move.

Afraid to break the spell.

I've never had a sweeter kiss, and for the first time, I understand what it means to be in love with someone.

Realizing I love Clara sparks a knot of anxiety that grips my stomach.

My heart knows what it wants, but will she want more than what we have?

A stark realization hits me hard as I gather her in my arms, and she rests her head on my chest. I never want to kiss anyone but Clara Dean Sharp.

Chapter 40

Clara

The designs are finished, and Abigail has a big reveal scheduled for this afternoon. I glance around the cabin and sigh. Archer will love this place. It's perfect for the inn he decided to open, rustic yet stylish. He already has a manager spot listed online and has been working on a name for it.

I'm currently sitting on a plush leather sofa in a guest suite pretending to watch Jane redo the decorations on the fireplace.

The prospect of seeing Archer again sends shivers

coursing through my blood. He went back to Little Rock the morning after our movie night, which left me confused. But he said he had something important to do. I hope it's not to see Brianna. I mean, why would it be?

Why didn't I ask him about her the other night? Trevor's voice keeps playing in my head. Taunting me. I don't believe Archer is engaged. I know he's not. And he's undoubtedly not going to ask me. At least not yet. Maybe someday?

When Trevor asked me to marry him, I was happy. I thought I was in love and that he loved me too. But what I felt for Trevor pales in comparison to my feelings for Archer. In the words of Bella Swan, I am unconditionally and irrevocably in love with him.

This is far from the crush I had on football player Archer. Yes, I thought he was gorgeous and stunning, and I crushed on him so hard. I admit I flew to Vegas just to see him play.

I had it bad.

Now, I love him.

Does he feel the same about me?

"Clare Bear?" Jane snaps her fingers and giggles. "You're in a lovesick daze."

"I won't deny it," I say before shoving a pillow over my face and screaming into it.

She glances at her forty-year-old Timex watch. "You'll see him in a few minutes. I dare you to walk up and kiss him when he gets here."

My heart skips a beat as I picture doing what Jane suggests. "No way."

"I would if I were you." She takes a step back from the fireplace and taps her chin.

I shake my head and glance at the fireplace. "I think the candles need to be moved to the other end."

She moves them and lands a hand on her hip before meeting my gaze. "You just better let him know you're interested."

"I'll find another way. I heard that Chance left last night for Arizona," I say, hoping to change the subject. I need to focus before Archer gets here, so I'm prepared *not* to kiss him like a fool.

I breathe a sigh of relief when Jane rolls with the subject change. "Yeah, he called me, and we agreed we like each other, but it's not love."

"Y'all could've fooled me."

"I've decided to take a break from dating for a while."

"You sure about that? I mean, the way Donny was flirting with you at the hospital has me thinking I could set the two of you up. It definitely seemed like there was some chemistry there," I say, jiggling my eyebrows. "And your face turned blood red."

"I am not dating your brother," Jane furrows her brow and uses her serious tone. "He's three years younger than me!"

"Archer is three years older than me. What if he refused to date a younger woman?"

"That's different and you know it."

"Okay, but Donny will be devastated."

"Shut up, punk," she says before checking her vibrating phone. "Mom wants us downstairs."

My heart falls with a bang, settling in my already knotted stomach. He's here. I imagine taking Jane's advice, and that makes my stomach roll with nausea. I rush past a laughing Jane and stop near the entrance where Abigail stands.

As soon as the door opens, Archer smiles at me. With his black slacks and purple button-up, his eyes pop like the ocean in Destin on a sunny day. He looks like the ultimate billionaire CEO, and I'm not sure if my heart can take it. He stops in front of me, my lungs are bathed in woodsy pine mixed with crisp, clean goodness.

Jane skips by, stopping close to Archer's ear and loudly whispers, "You better kiss her because she's too chicken."

Apparently, Archer is good at taking directions. He runs his right hand down my cheek and presses a brief yet sweet kiss to my forehead. My heart pounds in my chest harder than it ever has. He leans back, and I'm lost in his eyes. "Hi," he says.

"Hi," I whisper.

Out of nowhere, he goes full CEO on me as his gaze sweeps the inn. I follow his line of sight, knowing he likes what he sees.

The entrance opens to the left, leading to a rustic front desk that was handmade by Urban Forge. All the furniture came from them and is not only one of a kind but is of exquisite craftsmanship.

To the right is a sitting area featuring a leather sofa and two burnt orange side chairs, accompanied by a coffee table, all of which surround a rock fireplace with a TV perched above. If you continue walking, it opens into a cozy dining area.

Paul slaps Archer on the back. "What do you think,

son?"

"Abigail and team, you all brought a vision I didn't even know I had to life. This is perfect."

After touring the rest of the inn, we show them the downtown office space, which is also a hit.

♥

After a dinner to celebrate, we decide to walk around downtown. Archer takes my hand and tugs me close. "Can I talk to you in private?"

I manage a nod since I've apparently lost my voice.

We walk down the square until we reach the bench where we had our almost first kiss that night. He looks at it and then at me before sitting down. "I fell for you that night we sat here drinking coffee."

My throat nearly closes off, and I can't speak.

He pulls a box out of his pocket and continues, "I went home this week to get this."

That can't be. No. I'm being silly.

He opens the box, and it is. Inside the box, a massive ring that must be three carats shines. "I know it's early, but I can't help it. I'd be honored if you would marry me."

Trevor's words echo in my head.

You don't think he'll marry you, do you? Because it would only be to stay CEO. I hope you realize that.

I drop my head into my hands. "I knew this would happen. I knew it!"

Archer cocks his head. "Clara? I'm asking you to marry me." The hurt on his face is nearly my undoing, but I have to stand my ground.

If Archer isn't in love with me, what would keep him from cheating? Once upon a time, mom loved dad. And she cheated.

"I get the question. But what I want to know is why. What is the real reason?" I now have Trevor's words on replay in my head.

Archer rubs the bridge of his nose and looks at me. "This isn't the way it's supposed to go. After I proposed, you were supposed to say yes. Then we would," he stops and swallows, looking at the ground.

"We would what? Run your company together?" Why am I so angry? Because the thing is, I know, without a doubt, I *want* to marry Archer. I can imagine having little football playing babies running around the house. Our daughter with big blue eyes, wrapping her daddy around her finger. I can picture a teenage

Archer lookalike sitting on the couch cheering on his favorite football team.

Saying yes right now would be so easy.

He drags his gaze to mine. "Kiss. We would kiss."

Just like that first night on the bench, I stand and run as fast as I possibly can.

Chapter 41

Archer

Well, that could've gone better. I slip the ring into my pocket and run after Clara. "Hey, will you stop?" I ask when I catch up.

She stops so suddenly I almost collide with her. The sky turns dark just as thunder booms in the distance. Sheets of rain pour down from the sky.

She whips around, her chest heaving up and down like she just finished a 10k. Her eyes narrow, and she stares at me, rain dripping down her face. As I look into her eyes, I realize not only did it not go as I expected, but it went way worse. She looks furious, which makes my blood simmer.

"I'm sorry if my proposal offended you," I say, wiping rain away from my eyes.

With a rough laugh, she closes her eyes and shakes her head. "Why did you propose to me?"

"I'm beginning to wonder the same thing." I lash out, my feelings hurt.

More laughter. "Do you think anything could ever tempt me to say yes to a marriage of convenience?" The rain doesn't seem to affect her at all.

My forehead creases as some of the anger deflates. "What are you talking about?"

Lightning cracks in the dark navy sky, fitting for the situation I find myself in. "What happened? Did Brianna turn you down?" she asks.

"Huh?"

"I already know you have to marry or lose your company."

"What does that have to do with anything?" The minute I ask the question, I know the answer. Clara assumed I was only asking to keep my position at Lombardi. Brianna must've told that little scumbag Trevor.

She crosses her arms and pins me with her gaze. "We haven't known each other long enough for you to propose."

"I disagree." My clothes are so drenched they stick to my body.

"I have an interview for a job in Alabama anyway, so I may not be here much longer."

My mouth falls open, and I stare at her in stunned silence as Jane pulls up in her Jeep. "What are y'all doing? It's raining!"

Clara meets my gaze before running to Jane's jeep and climbing inside. Jane drives away, leaving me in the rain feeling more alone than ever.

I walk into my freshly remodeled log cabin, and Dad glances at me from the couch in the lounge area, a big smile on his face. "Son, you were supposed to text so I could have your candlelight dinner ready."

His smile fades to a frown when he sees my haggard face. "Oh no."

"Clara's dad was right. She said no," I say, stripping my wet shirt off. I'd asked for her parent's permission to marry her. They gave it, but Anthony said she would say no.

"I was hoping her mom was right. I do agree she loves you. So, what did she say exactly?"

"She asked why I proposed."

"Did you say because you love her and want to be with her always?"

I wince. "Not exactly."

"What exactly did you say?"

My eyes close, and I make a sour face, embarrassed to recall my words. "I said I was beginning to wonder the same thing. I was a jerk."

"And then she said no?"

"Basically, she said she wouldn't marry for convenience, and she asked if Brianna turned me down."

"Get into some different clothes. We're watching Pride and Prejudice."

"What? Why would we watch that? Isn't it a girl's show?"

"I was planning to watch it this weekend but now is a better time. It's Abigail and Clara's favorite movie."

"Fine, but I expect a hot coffee waiting for me if you can figure out how to work the cappuccino machine."

He waves his hand. "I know how."

Four hours later, I've told Dad every detail about my relationship with Clara, and he's on board to help me win her heart. After the movie ends, I grab a piece of paper and start on a letter to Clara.

Yes, a letter.

Desperate times call for desperate measures.

Chapter 42

Clara

It's hard to believe Archer proposed to me last night, and now I'm at Tammy's wedding with dad. But I needed to take my mind off things, and what better way than a wedding?

"I'm happy to present Mr. and Mrs. Jace Eubanks," the preacher says, with a smile.

As Tammy and Jace walk hand in hand, I can't help but think how beautiful their kids would be. Even though Tammy is older, it's not out of the question.

At the reception, a blonde woman speaks in a loud

voice. "It's about time! Young people, if Jace and Tammy can find their way back to one another after all they went through, you can also find love."

Ruby shakes her head. "Lorene."

"What? I'm just trying to be encouraging."

Ruby claims an empty seat beside me. "Lorene is somewhat harmless, just loud."

"That's okay," I say as curiosity creeps into my mind. "What did she mean?"

"Tammy and Jace were high school sweethearts until he married someone else."

"Oh?"

"He had his reasons, but anyway, his wife passed away a few years ago, and he and Tammy ran into each other last year."

"Wow. I wonder how she forgave him."

"Love."

"Love?"

"It's what makes the world go round. If you truly love someone, don't let them go."

I glance at my traitor of a dad. He spoke with Archer and knew he was proposing, yet didn't say anything. He's not so quiet now. "I agree with Ruby."

On the drive home, Dad drums his fingers on the

steering wheel. He looks at me, then quickly turns his head. After three times, I sigh. "When are you going to tell me you and Mom are back together?"

His Adam's Apple bobs. "I was, well, um, going to see what you think about it."

"I'm fine with it, but Dad, it doesn't matter what I think," I say, sipping my cherry limeade.

"Yes, it does," he replies, leaning forward with the same earnest look I've seen many times from the countless heart-to-heart conversations we've had over the years. "Your mom and I love you; your approval would mean a lot. Your blessing, even."

I nearly choke on my drink. "Blessing?" I ask as the lime fizzes up my nose.

"Yes."

After a few seconds, I swallow. "You have it," I say, meaning it, which surprises me.

A playful smile tugs at Dad's lips. "That was too easy. What's the catch?"

I take a moment to stare at the scenery as we drive out of Pocahontas, allowing myself a moment before answering. "I love y'all, and you deserve to be happy."

"Wow," he says, his expression softening. "Thank you, peanut."

Even though it's almost ten at night, as soon as we walk into the house, Gramma is brimming with excitement. She waves a letter in the air. "Clara Dean, you have mail, honey!"

"Okay," I say, more in the form of a question.

"Get over here and open it before I do," she says, shaking the letter at me before lowering her voice like we're sharing a secret. "It's from Archer."

I bound across the room and take the letter, ripping it open.

Dear Clara,

I want to clear up some things from our conversation last night since there was a bit of confusion. First off, I want to clarify the idea that I had asked Brianna to marry me before talking to you is completely untrue. I've never even considered asking her.

I want to assure you that my decision to propose was driven by genuine love. Although I have focused primarily on the company and my aspirations of returning to football, my feelings for you developed in a way I didn't anticipate. The deep love I have for you caught me off guard in the best possible way!

My proposal was also not motivated by my position.

Dad and I decided he will resume the role of CEO and I will support him, which will allow me to get back to the game I love while still helping and supporting the company.

Unlike Mr. Darcy, I fully intend to express my love and renew the sentiments which you had no interest in hearing last night. I believe and hope you will change your mind after reading this. I'll drop this letter off with your wonderful Gramma as soon as possible, since I know you are at a wedding.

I will wait for you, Clara. No matter how long it takes.

Yours forever,
Archer

I fold the letter before sliding onto the couch by Gramma. "He says he loves me and wants to marry me for me."

"And why shouldn't he?" Gramma asks, her tone full of confidence.

"Dad and I agree with Gramma," Mom says.

The moment I picture Archer walking away from me and into someone else's arms, my heart spasms with spikes of pain. That cannot happen. "I have to go," I say as I stand.

"You go get that man," Gramma makes a fist like she's punching the air.

Giggles flow from me as I drive toward the cabin. I hope Archer is there. Because I'm definitely getting my man.

Chapter 43

Archer

I know Clara was at her cousin's wedding, but my nerves are on edge waiting to hear from her. What if she decides she truly doesn't like me that much? Maybe her feelings are tied to the persona of Archer Banks, the football star. And what if she doesn't care for the man?

Could I be like Mr. Darcy and walk away from the woman I love? Not that he had to in the end, so maybe that's how our story will go.

Should I walk outside and wait for Clara to join

me like Mr. Darcy joined Elizabeth? I've watched that movie three times in the past twenty-four hours. Simply because it's Clara's favorite and watching it makes me feel close to her. I know, I'm weird.

I've never been in love. This is so new, and I don't know how to act. But I finally have a chance at true happiness and don't want to lose it. Yes, sure, I've been happy playing on the field. I've been blessed to have my parents and my grandfatherrents. I was raised by loving people. Is it too much to want a love like what I feel for Clara?

Car lights flash through the window. I rise from the couch so fast I trip on the area rug and fall into one of two accent chairs before clanking my knee on the coffee table. Pain shoots through my knee as I limp toward the door, swinging it open.

Clara's eyes widen, and she lowers her hand to her side. "I was just about to knock," she says, tucking a loose curl behind her ear.

Her green eyes are full of love, and I hear myself invite her inside.

She lowers onto the couch and turns to me when I sit beside her. "When did you watch Pride and Prejudice?"

"Once last night and twice today," I admit, my cheeks flushing slightly as Clara looks into my eyes.

"Why so many times?" she asks, a hint of surprise in her voice.

"Honestly," I say, taking a deep breath, "because I feel so much closer to you when I watch it."

Her green eyes double in size before she lowers her gaze. "Archer, I'm sorry for the way I acted when you proposed."

"I understand why you may have felt the way you did. Please believe I've fallen in love with you," I continue, my voice steady but filled with emotion, hoping she can hear the sincerity behind my words. "My one wish is to be your husband. I don't care where we work or what we do as long as we're together."

She draws in a sharp breath. "I've thought you were adorable since I saw you squirt some Gatorade in your mouth almost six years ago. You were standing on the sidelines, and your hair was blowing, and you looked sweaty, but your eyes mesmerized me."

"How do you feel about me now?" I lean in closer, the warmth of our breath mixing together, as anticipation courses through me.

With a gentle smile playing on her lips, she looks

into my eyes as if weighing the moment. "You stole my heart in Mountain View, with the way you handled getting sprayed by a skunk and then that spontaneous picnic by the lake. Not to mention the way you've made me laugh until I cried. I've known for a while that I love you."

A surge of hope blossoms in my chest, spreading warmth through my veins. "Does that mean what I think it does?"

She nods, her gaze steady and filled with sincerity. "The answer is yes. I will marry you, Archer Briggs Banks."

With a whoop, I pull Clara up into my arms. The pain in my knee fades from my mind as I stand, swirling her around like an airplane, just like my dad used to do with me. Her delighted yelp fills the air, and I can already picture the laughter and fun awaiting us in our upcoming adventures together.

"I know what I'm going to name this place," I say as warmth spreads up my arm and into my heart.

"What?" She leans back, her lashes beating softly as she gazes into my eyes.

"Stargazer's Inn." The name feels right. My gaze caresses hers, and I feel so much love for her I can hardly contain it.

A blush pinkens her cheeks as her arms tighten around my waist. "I like it. What made you choose that name?"

"Because all my wishes have come true right here in this moment." My breath hitches a little as I allow Clara to see a vulnerable side of me. A side not many have seen.

She reaches out and runs her hand down my face, a glimmer of unshed tears sparkling on her lids. "I love you so much."

"And I love you, my Clara."

My lips brush her ear and cheek before she meets my eyes, and we pause. Her lashes flutter as her soft-as-silk gaze ensnares me. A bubbly sensation fills my heart, and I can no longer contain myself. I brush a long curl away from her neck, and she sighs, leaning into my hand. I move closer until our mouths are almost touching. I smile, wanting to savor every touch. When our lips meet, I think my heart may jump out of my chest. It's beating harder than ever, even more than during my most stressful football game.

I already know this is going to be a very short engagement.

Epilogue

Clara

The football stadium is packed solid. I stand and scream as my husband, yes, I said husband, has the ball and is running across the field with all he has.

My heart pounds harder the closer he gets to scoring a touchdown. I can barely hear myself think over Gramma, Donny, Mom, and Dad's loud mouths. I think they're yelling louder than I am. Not to mention Abigail and Paul.

A player from the other team makes a jump for Archer, but he moves to the left just in time to score a touchdown. I yell before lowering myself into my seat.

Donny grips my hand. "They won!"

I'm working hard to register the fact that Archer's team just made it to the Super Bowl—the *Super Bowl!*

My phone vibrates, and I accept a FaceTime call from Jane. She appears on the screen, her long hair crimped, and a part of it pulled up in a turquoise scrunchie.

"I wish you were here." I pout.

"You know I'd love to be there," Jane says. "But I never thought I'd be a part of this competition!"

I'm thrilled Jane was selected as a finalist in an interior design competition. It started last week, so she had to miss the game. Since Chance moved away, she has embraced being happily single and is focused on advancing her career.

After Jane and I end our call, I glance at my family with a contented smile. Since graduating from college, Donny has let his hair grow out, and he looks more like a rock star than ever. I suppose the fact that he and his band have been traveling around playing gigs for the last six months is working in his favor.

Abigail and Paul are still dating, which surprises

Archer. She's the first woman he's stayed with for more than a few months since losing Archer's mom.

Speaking of moms, mine is making goo-goo eyes at my dad. It's gross. Since they remarried three months ago, they can't keep their hands off each other.

Thankfully, Trevor left Lombardi Enterprises and is now working for a technology company. I don't know which one, nor do I care.

As for me and Archer? We're married and living in Vegas. He's back on the team as quarterback, and I'm still a freelance designer. Life couldn't be better.

My insides swish, and I giggle. Did I say life couldn't be better? I press my hand to my stomach. There's a chance it may be better. I'll know in a few days.

Mom narrows her eyes. "You good?"

"I'm great, Mom. Never better."

She leans into my ear and whispers, "I want to be called Gigi."

I gasp and meet her sparkling eyes. "What? How?"

"I'm a doctor, but most importantly, a mom. We know things."

"Don't say anything," I say as I lean my head on her shoulder.

"Not a peep." She rests her chin on the top of my

head.

Three days later, a pink line appears on the home test. I rush from the bathroom and stop in front of Archer, who's watching Persuasion for the second time this week. I believe I've turned him into a Jane Austen superfan.

"Do you want to have a boy or a girl?"

He pauses the movie and grins at me. "I'll take either. Why? Are you...?"

I suck my bottom lip between my teeth and nod.

He bolts off the couch and stops in front of me. "Clara Dean Banks, are you pregnant?"

"It's not official, but..." I pull the test from behind my back.

He picks me up and dances around the room. "This is better than going to the Super Bowl!" he says, laughter pouring from him.

We laugh together for a minute before I start crying happy, happy tears. Archer kisses the tears away from my cheeks before moving to my lips for the best kiss of my life.

━━━━━ ♥ ━━━━━

If you enjoyed *__Love Inn The View,__* please consider leaving a review. Thank you so much!

Afterword

Did you enjoy hearing about the places Archer and Clara visited? Many of the locations in this book are real places and businesses in Mountain View. Have you ever been to any of these spots? I'm here and would love to hear about your experience! What are your thoughts... did I capture the essence? Let me know!

Facebook page @writingleahbrewer
Website www.theleahjournal.com
Email: leahbrewerauthor@gmail.com

Check these places out:
- Blanchard Springs Caverns and Recreation Area 704 Blanchard Springs Road, Fifty-Six, AR 72533 www.blanchardsprings.org

- Both The Skillet Restaurant and

Ozark Folk Center can be found at https://www.arkansasstateparks.com/parks/ozark-folk-center-state-park

- Mountain View Music https://www.facebook.com/MountainViewMusicStore

- Sasquatch Cave 108 West Main Street, Mountain View, AR 72560 (870) 269-6800 SasquatchCave.MV@gmail.com

- Stone Drive In Theatre 808 Theatre Lane, Mountain View, AR 72560 Phone (Schedule Recording): (870) 269-3227 htttp:// stonedrivein.net

- The Inn at Mountain View 307 W Washington St., Mountain View, AR (870) 269 4200 https://innatmv.com/

- Urban Forge https://urbanforge.com/

- Johnny Cash's boyhood home https://dyesscash.astate.edu/

Coming Soon

If you enjoyed Clara's story, stay tuned for Jane's story next. I hope you enjoy the free preview that may be changed a bit after my editor gets ahold of it!

Chapter 1

I've never known a more incompetent burglar. Although I haven't met or known many burglars, this one takes the cake.

"Ma'am?" The 911 operator's calm voice interrupts my train of thought. "Police are on the way, please stay on the line."

"Look, I know it's going to take them at least fifteen

minutes to get here. I'm going to find a weapon."

"Please don't engage. Just hide."

"I'm sorry, but I've got to go." I slip my phone into my cousin, Shawna's, hand. "Hold this while I look for a weapon."

Whoever is downstairs crashes into what sounds like the table I moved from behind the sofa to the foyer yesterday.

Glass shatters.

The burglar yelps.

Yikes, they must've knocked the lamp off the table.

My mind races. Did I forget to set the alarm? Could the bumbling burglar be smart enough to have disabled it? Will the police get here in time?

I creep down the dark stairway, with Shawna on my heels. "Who do you think it is, Jane?" she whispers.

"Hush, I need to listen," I whisper back before I stop at the door that leads to the open concept kitchen and living area.

Not only am I at a secluded lake house at midnight, but I'm here alone with my younger cousin. I glance around the dark area since I don't dare turn the light on. My gaze lands on the iron skillet I used to make potatoes earlier. I quickly wrap my fingers around the handle and motion for Shawna to follow me into the pantry. I'm thankful the pantry is close to the door by the staircase.

Whoever is in here just ran into the couch I'd recently rearranged. I can see their outline. At least it's just one person. A man based on his size. The man moans before continuing across the room.

My weapon is ready.

I'm ready.

The burglar has no idea what's coming. He crept into the wrong lake house. Not only is he about to face a skillet, but the person holding it has played almost as many baseball games as Nolan Ryan.

Not to mention, I can swing a bat faster than most men.

And I'm a woman.

Leaning close to Shawna's ear, I lower my voice as much as possible. "Stay here. I'm stepping into the living room to see who this is."

"Okay." She sounds brave, but I detect a bit of fear in her voice.

Now, I'm aggravated. How dare someone come into my best friend's lake house and try to rob it and scare my cousin in the process.

They probably think the place is empty since Clara lives in Las Vegas with her famous football player husband. I'm only staying here because I'm in a design competition in the next town over.

What if someone saw me and Shawna and wants to kidnap us? A trickle of fear runs down my spine, followed by a surge of determination.

No way will I let them take me or Shawna.

My grip tightens on the handle, and I raise the skillet like I'm up next to bat. I spread my legs and get ready to knock the robber out.

A dark shadow crosses over the wall behind me. I'm hidden behind the massive dining cabinet. It's the perfect spot to ambush the robber.

Come a little closer. Just a few more steps, buddy, and you're meeting your Maker.

The footsteps stop.

I lunge from my hiding spot and swing the bat, er, the skillet. It hits them! Yes! Take that, robber!

Before I make another move, the skillet gets snatched from my hand, and the burglar presses me against the wall. Hard.

Shawna screeches as she bolts out of the pantry. "Get off my cousin!" she says right before she jumps on the robber's back.

Oh no, not Shawna!

I flip the light on, and the scene before me is not what I expected.

Shawna is pummeling the chest of none other than Donny Sharp, my best friend's annoying younger brother.

His green eyes sparkle as he smirks at me. "Now, Jane, if you wanted to get up close and personal with me, all you had to do was ask."

Shawna stands up, her face red as the blood flowing from Donny's hand.

Wait. Blood?

"What happened?" I ask, like I've lost my marbles.

He grins. "I think you broke my finger with that stupid skillet, there, Chuck Norris."

Blue lights surround us before footsteps stomp onto the wrap-around porch. "Police! Open up!"

With a sigh, I lean my head back and stare at the ceiling. There's no way I'm ever going to live this down.

Acknowledgments

Writing a book is an exhilarating journey that takes a lot of time and energy, and I couldn't have done it alone! I've been incredibly lucky to have an amazing support system cheering me on every step of the way.

A big thank you to my wonderful daughter, Carissa, and my dear friend, Melinda, for spending countless hours exploring Mountain View and its surroundings with me, diving deep into research. I've cherished every moment of our adventures together!

To my fantastic BETA readers, Vickie and Regina —wow, you both are absolute rockstars! Your feedback and encouragement have always been invaluable.

To my husband, Mark, my daughter, Cassidy, and my son-in-law, Logan, thank you for being here for me! Cassidy, your feedback greatly helped with the cover design and the final product. I can't thank you enough!

And I can't forget my incredibly talented illustrator, Nicole Roush! Thank you for working on our Clara and Archer until they were perfect!

I want to give a heartfelt shout-out to Mrs. Judy! Her own love story truly touched me and served as a wonderful source of inspiration for Gramma's beautiful tale that she shared with Archer. Thank you, Mrs. Judy, for letting your experiences shine through and enrich our narrative!

Stephanie, you always find a way to make my words so much better!

I would also like to extend my heartfelt thanks to the warm and welcoming community in Mountain View. A special shoutout to Kenny and Cheri at The Inn at Mountain View, as well as the amazing folks from Sasquatch Cave, Stone Drive-In Theatre, and Mountain View Music. You all have made this journey unforgettable!

About the Author

Leah Brewer has written nine novels, a children's book, and several short stories. She also shares Christian articles on her blog, with almost fifty under her belt. Leah lives in Arkansas with her husband and family. She can't really get going until she's had her morning coffee—let's be real, that's a must! A trip to the beach brings her nearly as much joy as hanging out with her family. Romance is a big part of all her books, and she feels that stories really helped her heal after being diagnosed with ovarian cancer in 2019. Thankfully, she's been cancer-free for six years now! Leah enjoys writing happy-ever-after tales, aiming to make readers smile, strengthen their relationship with God, and help them find their happy place.

Check her out online at facebook.com/writingleahbrewer or at www.theleahjournal.com.